*To Bennett –*
*Hope you enjoy the*
*outdoor adventures!*
*Fish On,*
*K.J. Houtman*

# SPARE THE ROD

### By K.J. Houtman

D1446132

This book is dedicated to professional anglers.
Live the dream.

Fish On Kids Books LLC
P.O. Box 3
Crystal Bay, MN 55323-0003

Website address: www.fishonkidsbooks.com

Library of Congress Control Number: 2010939203

ISBN: 9780982876022

Other works by K.J. Houtman
*A Whirlwind Opener*
&
*Driving Me Crazy*

FIRST EDITION 2010

Manufactured in the United States of America

# Chapter 1

"Please?" Jake's voice carries a twinge of whine, which doesn't go over very well at the dinner table. Gus looks the other way, not sure if Mom or Dad will pounce.

The clink of silverware on plates fills the silence as the five of them, counting Pops, finish their meal. Jim and Annie aren't usually the pouncing type, but Jake's on a little thin ice. Out of the corner of his eye, Gus sees them exchange a glance, then a nod.

"All right, you can drive your mother's car tomorrow. We'll carpool, but promise you'll drive down to get her if I need you to, after school, in case I'm running late. You have an appointment tomorrow?" Jim is a freelance photographer that does a lot of work in the hunting and fishing industries. Photo shoots don't always go smoothly, and sometimes can take longer than expected.

Annie nods her head, affirming.

"Promise. No problem." Jake is quick with his answer, hiding a brief panic over the thought of having to drive into downtown Minneapolis by himself to pick up his mom, if needed. City driving is a still a little bit intimidating for a 16-year-old, who's only had his driver's license a few weeks.

"Can I ride with Jake to school tomorrow since he's taking your car, Mom? I've got some stuff in my locker that I need to bring home." Gus doesn't have nearly the volume in the bottom of his locker as Jake does. Jake accumulates junk all year long. That's the big reason he wanted the car for the last day of school tomorrow. No way he wanted to bring all that home on the bus.

"Sure. But be careful with your brother in the car, Jake." Moms

3

are wired to worry, but Jake's a good driver.

"SWEET! That's great." Gus pumps his fist in the air, thankful that he doesn't have to ride the bus with Matt Driver. His year of reprieve arrives a day early. Gus has been counting down for weeks now, knowing that he gets a break not just for the summer, but for the entire school year next year. Matt Driver is a year older, finishing sixth grade and going into seventh grade. That means Driver will be riding the high school bus and attending junior high, while Gus is a year behind, going into sixth. Gus can't wait for a break from him for awhile.

The boys exchange a knowing look. Jake knows how much trouble Driver has been for his little brother and a few other people. Maybe Matt Driver won't be bugging as many people as he used to.

"I found something else out that I think you'll like, Gus," Dad smiles as he says it.

"What's that, Dad?"

"That team walleye tournament you wanted to do—the Masters?"

"Is that the one you have to be 12 for?" Pops asks. Pops is Annie's dad and lives with the family.

"Yeah?" Gus looks a little grumpy about this. He wants to start his career in fishing...now. Unfortunately, he has to be 12 and fish with a guardian. He doesn't turn that until September 11th, by then all the tournaments are finished up for the year except the Championships, and you have to earn your way into those. He'll have to wait until next summer, and that sticks in his craw, as Pops would say.

"Was talking with Johnnie Candle about their west division, and it sounds like there's a tournament the 18th and 19th of September."

"Really?" Dad has Gus' attention now. Those dates mean he'll be 12 and eligible. "How much, could we do it?"

"It is pretty expensive." Jim tells the family how much the entry fee is. "Add hotel, eating out, out-of-state fishing license, bait and gas—both for the truck and the boat." He offers up a grand total.

"Whew-doggie," whistles Pops. "That's a lotta enchiladas."

"That IS a lot of money," Gus says with a sigh, unaware (until now) of how many zeroes were in the fishing tournament idea.

"But don't worry, son," Dad continues. "We'll split it. I'll pay my half and you pay your half. That's how team tournaments work, and then we split any winnings 50/50." Dad smiles at Mom.

"Too bad you're too young to work at Rockvam," Jake offers. That's where he works. Jake helps cashier in the store, cleans up boats that they rent out and helps customers at the gas dock. His favorite part is gassing up the big yachts on Lake Minnetonka. Sometimes he gets sweet tips, like five, 10 or 20 bucks.

"Yeah, I don't have that kind of money."

"You'll figure something out." Mom is always hopeful.

"I really want to do it, Dad. I just don't have the cash right now."

"That's okay. I understand. No pressure. We have until August to figure out whether we want to get in or not. It's on Lake Waubay in South Dakota, a fun little lake just loaded with walleyes, only four hours from here." The Roberts family lives on Lake Minnetonka, just west of Minneapolis.

"That helps." How is Gus going to get that much money put together in just three months? Come to think of it, somebody owes him forty bucks.

# Chapter 2

"Thanks Gus, really. Here's your money back." Marsha gives Gus an envelope at his locker the next morning, Katie is just two lockers down and listening in on the transaction. Both Marsha and Katie have been a lot happier this last week. "You-know-who gave it back to me yesterday after school. I didn't see you on the bus this morning or you'd have it sooner."

"I rode with my brother today. He drove the car. I'm glad you got the money back, Marsha."

"Me too. He's been so much better, not bugging me at all lately, just ignoring me." The trio knows who they are talking about, even if anyone eavesdropping wouldn't. Matt Driver was really giving Marsha a hard time, but hopefully, that's all in the past now.

"Good. That's the way it should be."

"I don't know what you did or said, Gus, but he's much better."

"Don't worry about it, Marsha. But if he bothers you again—or anyone else, just let me know."

"Okay." Marsha looks over at Katie. "And thank you, too, Katie."

"No problem. I'm glad we found a solution, right Gus?"

"Yeah, see you. Gotta go or I'll be late."

"Bye, Marsha," Katie says as she and Gus walk to Mrs. Kaye's classroom. "I really liked your journal, Gus. Turning it in today?"

"Yup. Right now." He puts the soft brown leather journal, his recent constant companion, in Mrs. Kaye's wire basket on the left corner of her desk. "You turning in your story I read last week?"

"I turned it in on Friday."

"I liked your story, Katie. Thanks for letting me read it."

The bell rings just after the two arrive in their seats. Ah, the last day of school, and only a half-day to boot. It is a lazy fun day: cleaning out desks, closets, shelves and lockers; turning in text books, checking off lists. Gus enjoys a checklist and is happy to help Mrs. Kaye get everything inventoried. It's a lot of fussing on details, but not a lot of school work. Soon the whole school is outside on this beautiful June day for recess at the same time. The P.E. teachers have all the balls outside. ALL the balls, and there still aren't enough for everyone.

"Hi, Gus," Mr. Limmer's working supervision on the playground, and was Gus' favorite teacher last year in fourth grade.

"Hey there. How's your latest whittling project?" Mr. Limmer is always working on carving something, most often wooden Santas that are fishing or hunting. Annie has bought one every year at the local craft show. She says they are works of art.

"It's pretty good. I've been working on an osprey in the nest."

"You're carving osprey? Wow."

"Yeah, it's a little tricky. I'm trying to get one with the parent bringing in a fish to the nest of the hatchlings. Hard to get the wings looking realistic."

"I bet. Big project you're undertaking." Gus sees Matt Driver, who gives an ugly look his way, but doesn't say anything. He's busy batting balls around with a bat.

"I decided to kick it up a notch." Mr. Limmer is a talented whittler.

"Did you know that once the first osprey hatches, it can take several days for the rest of the eggs in an osprey nest to hatch? When that happens, the oldest hatchling hogs all the fish that the adult brings to the nest. They can really torment the younger hatchlings, sometimes to the point that they can't survive."

"Huh. I knew an osprey's main diet is fish, I didn't know the hatchlings fight over it." Mr. Limmer is always impressed with how many interesting little things Gus knows. "I know they always nest by bodies of water; a river or a lake, with a good source of fish."

Gus looks over at Matt Driver, and wonders if he's like the oldest osprey hatchling, making trouble for the younger ones. He can't stand not being the center of attention any longer. "C. Guuuu-stav

Roberts!"

Not again. Gus tries his best to ignore the big oaf, he had hoped this would be over. No luck, guess it only proves that Driver is unaware of exactly who paid him a visit last week when his folks were at the Twins game.

"Hey C. Gustav, is this your pretty pink ball?" Driver has a huge pink ball now, not a small red rubber ball. This is a therapy ball, the kind people do training and exercises; sitting and rolling on the ball. It's tall, almost waist high.

"I bet it's your favorite color, bright pink like bubble gum." Driver's on a roll, Gus and Mr. Limmer are looking his way, but Gus just tries to ignore him. "Let me pop that bubble for you, C. Gustav!" Not too long ago, Driver learned that Gus has a first name that starts with a "C." But he doesn't know what it is—yet. Thank goodness.

Driver winds up his baseball bat, but instead of whacking the ball away, they way he was doing with the small red rubber balls, he whacks it on the top. Only one problem, the bat bounces straight back and whacks Driver right between the eyes. Bulls-eye, middle of the forehead. With a moan, Driver is down on the ground, unsure what just happened.

Mr. Limmer rushes to his side. "Holy cow! Are you okay, Matt?"

"Ow, my head," Driver moans and cries. It starts to swell immediately, the bump red and hard. Gus can see it from where he stands, already the size of a small VW bug. He doesn't rush to Driver's side with Mr. Limmer, the teacher's got it under control. Besides, it's probably not a good idea for Driver to see the slight smirk on Gus' face right now. In fact, Gus should probably turn and leave.

Just as he's about to move Mr. Limmer calls out, "Gus, get me an ice pack, please."

"Yes, sir." Gus heads to the nurses office and secures the cold compress, giving himself a small moment of pleasure when the nurse asks what happened. "Matt Driver hit himself on the head with a baseball bat. Seriously." Couldn't have happened to a better guy.

# Chapter 3

"What happened to Matt Driver?" Katie wants to know, catching up to Gus on the way in from recess. "Somebody said you hit him with a baseball bat."

Gus' mouth drops open. "I didn't touch him. He hit HIMSELF with a baseball bat."

"What? How can you do that?"

"I don't know, he's talented."

"He has a tomato growing out of his forehead."

"Kinda looks like it."

"You really didn't hit him?"

"Nope, he really did it all by himself. Ask Mr. Limmer, he watched him do it."

"Wow. Impressive." The two share a moment as they walk back into the school, heading to Mrs. Kaye's classroom.

"Okay, class," Mrs. Kaye addresses the sea of surliness with just one hour left to go in the school year. "Make sure your lockers are all cleaned out. Here are some paper bags if you need them to organize what to pitch and what to take home. Get it done, everyone. Let's go!"

Gus walks with the group as they disperse with brown-handled paper bags in tow toward the hallway. However, his locker is already cleaned out, he even scrubbed it with 409.

"Hi, Gus. You got a minute?" Mrs. Kaye calls out as he wanders by her desk.

"Sure." Uh-oh, did he do anything wrong? "Don't believe the

rumors you hear, ma'am." Might as well be proactive.

"What rumors, Gus?"

"That I hit Matt Driver with a baseball bat. I didn't. He did it all by himself, just ask Mr. Limmer."

"Oh, that. I heard about that already. No, I wanted to compliment you on your journal assignment." She hands it back to him with an A+ on a post-it note on the cover, drawn with a fish and a smiley face.

"Thank you." Gus stands tall and smiles. Not one to be very worried about grades, Gus is proud of this one. He gets mostly As or Bs, whatever, it isn't really important to him. Sometimes school gets so boring that he doesn't pay attention, or really thinks an assignment is totally stupid and won't do it. But this? He worked hard on this journal over the last month and is happy with an A+.

"Did you enjoy writing? Journaling?"

"I liked it, a lot actually. I think I'd like to keep at it."

"That's great. There's still more empty pages, keep at it over the summer."

"I might just do that."

"Oh, and Gus?"

"Yes, ma'am?"

"You put a little magic in it."

Gus is not sure what to say to this nice teacher, always so encouraging and full of fun. She's a happy personality and hardly ever has a crabby day. He sure will miss her next year.

Soon the bell rings and there is a ton of commotion as everyone heads out. Time to meet up with Jake.


"Hey, Gus." It's Doogie and Asher walking out to the buses. Doogie hops on route 101 with a wave.

"Hi, Asher. Happy summer vacation." Doogie and Asher are best friends, and sometimes Gus makes a threesome.

"I'm so happy."

"Me too."

"Wanna hang out this afternoon, do some fishing?"

"I'd love to—but, I gotta do a project today."

"A project? On the last day of school? What's up with that?"

"I need a summer job, Asher. Need some mula."

"Saving up for a car already? What's the rush?"

"No, a fishing tournament in September."

"Huh?"

"It's a long story. I'll call you, we'll go soon, I promise." Gus hops in the front seat. Jake's at the wheel.

"Bye," Asher says to himself as he begins the six block walk to his house.

Jake has the tunes cranked up on the car stereo. He turns it down a little bit when Gus hops in. "What happened to Matt Driver? I saw him walk by and he looks like Pinocchio, only his nose was growing out of his forehead!"

"He did that to himself today, with a baseball bat." Gus replays the scene in his mind, watching the bat ricochet up from the big bouncy ball.

"No way."

"Seriously, Mr. Limmer and I watched it happen. He got a little lesson first hand on Newton's third natural law of physics." Gus chuckles thinking how for every action there is an equal and opposite reaction. "Lesson learned on the playground lab."

"Did he knock himself out?"

"No, but he was probably seeing stars."

"Or tweeting birds." Jake's thinking of a scene from Roger Rabbit. "Has he figured out who paid him a little visit last week?"

"Nope."

"Has he straightened up?"

"Yeah, he gave the money back to Marsha, and she says he hasn't given her a hard time at all."

"Good."

"But he's still a dweeb to me."

"You can handle it."

"Great."

The drive home is much less eventful than the last time the two boys were on this route. Coming home from a school play together, Jake got pulled over by the cops, with a speeding ticket as a souvenir. Jake wanted to keep it all a secret when it happened, but he spilled the beans, not Gus.

"Hey, congratulations, you're a Junior."

"Thanks, and you're a sixth grader. King-of-the-hill."

"Yup. You got plans for this afternoon?"

"Vids for a little while, then we're meeting at the beach and a group of friends are wakeboarding."

"Sounds fun."

"How about you, you going fishing I suppose?"

"No, I've got a project this afternoon."

"What, not fishing related? I can't believe it."

"I didn't say it wasn't fishing related, just said I wasn't fishing."

Pulling up to the house, Jake has to stay to the far right side on the driveway. The left side has a big pile of sand. Check that, HUGE pile of sand, with a wheelbarrow, rake, and a shovel nearby. A stick is perched at the top of the pile, piercing a piece of paper. There's writing on it.

"What is this?" Jake wonders out loud and slams the car door.

"I don't know. What does it say?"

Jake grabs the note. "Oh no," is all Gus hears from Jake, other than the moan.

*Jake,*

*Our lakefront has experienced too much erosion over the last few years. I applied for a permit to improve the shoreline with new rocks and sand and got permission. Here's a shovel, a rake, and a wheelbarrow along with 22 tons of sand. Move everything from here to the beach. After you are done, use the rake to smooth it all out.*

*Love,*

*Dad & Mom*

*P.S. Learn to watch your lead foot and do NOT hide things from your parents.*

Poor Jake. Twenty-two tons is a lot of sand.

# Chapter 4

"Hey." Gus greets Pops alone, as Jake is stuck in the driveway, either in awe of the daunting task ahead or wishfully willing it away. If only.

"Hey yourself." Pops is doing pretty great these days, considering, and Gus is glad to see it. He's had some small health scares, but is okay now.

"Chocolate cookie?"

"These are good, you made them today?" Gus replies with a mouthful.

"Yup. I get bored when no one else is around. Sides, I figured ya needed to celebrate the end of the scruel year." Pops has a way of talking that takes a little getting used to. School for him is scruel.

"Sorry about that. But you'll have us around a lot more for the summer."

"I'll go from too quiet to crazy with you boys around every day under my feet." Pops harrumphs.

Gus smiles at Pops. "You're just cranky 'cuz the Twins didn't play today." Pops listens or watches every single game.

"Maybe that's it."

"Where's Mom?"Usually if there isn't a game the odds are good that she'll be home that day. She works for the Minnesota Twins and is often at the games, entertaining corporate sponsors and taking them out to dinner, planning promotions. Most people think she has the best job in the world. Gus just knows he gives up a lot of his mom to baseball. She works a lot of nights and weekends.

"Doctor's appointment. Jimbo brought her home from the office early, since Jakey had the car and all."

"Thanks for the cookies. I've gotta go."

"What are you in such a hog's fire hurry over?"

"Gotta find a job, Pops. Gotta find a job."

Pops mutters something that Gus can't make out, sure it is something he doesn't really want to hear anyway. Figuring Pops out takes a little effort, but right now he has more important things on his mind. He heads out across the yard, to the big house with the beautifully landscaped yard.

"Hi, Mrs. Cavendish."

"Hello there. What's your name again? Co..."

"GUS, ma'am," he interrupts, quickly. Sheesh. "Gus Roberts, three doors down. Jim and Annie's youngest."

"Oh, Gus. I don't know why I thought your name was something else. Does Dr. Cavendish know that your name is Gus?"

"Yes, he's my pediatrician, ma'am. But sometimes my health records show my formal full name. I just go by Gus, though, ALL THE TIME. We can just keep the fact that I have another name a little secret between us, okay?"

"I totally get that, Gus. I hate my first name—everybody calls me Mickey. If they call me Viola, I'll give 'em what for."

Gus smiles. A kindred spirit.

"So," continues Mickey. "What can I do for you today, Gus?"

"I was wondering if you wanted help with some yard work this summer. Could I mow your lawn, do some trimming and edge work, weed the garden, rake the beach, paint the gazebo? Anything like that?"

"Hmm. I'm not sure. We have a lawn service that does most of that, and they do a good job."

"I bet they are expensive, though, ma'am."

"Well, you get what you pay for in life, I guess."

"True that. But what if I do some of the jobs that they don't do?"

"I admire your desire to work this summer, Gus. Too many kids these days just want to play and have fun, never taking on hard work. What do you need the money for?"

14

"My dad and I have a special adventure planned for September, and I have to come up with half to go along."

"A special adventure? Sounds fun."

"Do I have the job, Mrs. Cavendish? If I do, I'll tell you all about it. If not, I need to knock on some other doors. Time's a-wastin' as Pops would say."

"Mickey, please. Call me Mickey. If I hear 'Mrs. Cavendish' I turn around, looking for my mother-in-law." She rolls her eyes.

"My folks would kill me if I called you by your first name—or your nickname. If I don't want to clean out the garage all day on Saturday, I'd best just stick to Mrs. Cavendish."

"I can't do it, Gus. It makes me look over my shoulder for you-know-who."

"Well...how about Mrs. C? Would that work okay?"

"Oh all right. But Gus, Doc and I are kind of picky about our yard. You still have to do a good job. I won't pay you for lazy work."

"No ma'am." The two discuss the amount per hour and the projects she wants done first. She won't let the professional yard service go completely, she'll cut them back to every other week. Gus can fill in the off weeks, to see how it goes, starting this week. "Thank you. Can I start tomorrow?"

"Not a peep until nine o'clock, Gus. I love the early morning sounds of birds singing and wind in the trees during my coffee and quiet time in the morning. No work until nine o'clock at the earliest, 9:30 is even better."

"Yes, ma'am."

"But I paint in the afternoons, Gus, and I really can't have irritating noises while I'm trying to create. So done by noon."

"Done by noon? But starting after nine o'clock?"

"9:30 is better. Can you make that work? And no weekends. Doc is home on weekends."

"Yes, ma'am." Gus tries hard to not let the disappointment sound in his voice. "I've got a job working for my neighbor doing yard work. She's not giving me the hours I want, it's just every other week 9:30 to noon. I'll be more than half-way there by September."

# Chapter 5

Gus knocks on more neighbors' doors looking for work, but few are home. He'll have to try back in the evening. For now, a little lunch sounds like the ticket.

"Jakey, you want a sammich?" Pops hollers up the stairs.
"No thanks." The answer back, amongst loud music.
"Grilled cheese. You want one?"
"Sounds perfect." Gus helps get the bread, butter and cheese out, pours a glass of milk and opens a bag of chips.
"What's wrong with your brother?"
"You mean other than the 22 tons of sand in the driveway and his checkbook $135 lighter?"
"That is a ginormous amount of sand."
"True that. I wonder how long it will take him to move it."
"Forever at the rate he's going. It'll be good fer his muskels though." Pops is always encouraging Jake to spend more time in the weight room. He thinks a wrestler needs to be in tip top shape—with big strong muscles, and he's right of course. But Jake has a little bit of a lazy streak. He is a great wrestler already. He took State in his weight class this last year as a Sophomore. Pops loves wrestling.
"He'll get to it, Jake sometimes pushes things off."
"Tell me somethin' I don't know, buddy-roo."

After a couple of phone calls, Asher and Doogie come over to do some fishing afterall. Each boy brings his own rod and reel and a tackle box.

"You're so lucky to have this boat, Gus." Asher admires Gus' 15-foot fishing boat.

"My *Plywood Princess*?" Gus laughs, knowing they replaced the rotted pieces of wood on the seats with new plywood last year. They sit on throw cushions to avoid splinters.

"Yeah, I wish I had my own boat," Asher continues. "I'd be in it every day of the summer."

"I have had a lot of fun in this boat," Gus assures his friends. "It's not like I'm ungrateful or anything, but..."

"But what?"

"When I turn 12, I'll be able to drive that one." Gus points at his dad's Ranger 620 with a 225 horsepower Merc Opti, fully equipped with not just one, but two color Lowrance High-Definition GPS and Sonar units. "It's only three months away."

"Your dad sure has a sweet boat." Asher drools as he looks at the Ranger, secure in the lift at the end of the dock.

"I heard he's selling it," mentions Doogie. "Why's he doing that?"

"He's got a new one on order. He gets a new one every other year."

"Must be nice." Doogie says it with a little bit of whine.

"He gets a good deal on it, and he helps out the Ranger dealer with a lot of things that he needs, so it's a win-win." Gus is proud of his dad, Jim, and his work in the fishing and hunting industries. He's a professional photographer and does a lot of photo shoots for catalogs, ads, and magazine covers. He also guides for fishing some of the time. People know they can call him and trust him to host their friends and have a good time. He treats them right. He even does some videography for television.

"He's on their pro-staff, right?" Asher's been around their house enough to know the answer already.

"Yeah." Gus loads his St. Croix rod and two of his many tackle boxes into the boat.

"So he's a professional fisherman, right?" Doogie hops in with his stuff.

"I don't know. He guides some of the time, and he used to fish tournaments but hasn't for awhile."

"I think if you're on a company's pro-staff, you're a professional fisherman." Asher loads up his gear into the boat, and gives a shove off, away from shore.

"You think so?" Gus pulls the rip cord of the old Johnson 15-horse motor. On the 20th try, or maybe it just feels like 20, it takes off and Gus becomes the captain of the *Plywood Princess* for another outing. "Time to rock and roll." Gus high fives with Asher, who's sitting in the middle, who high fives with Doogie, in the front. The burnt orange *Plywood Princess* heads out on Lake Minnetonka for an afternoon of fun, heading to Crystal Bay. Gus has found an 18-foot shelf from his dad's GPS that he wants to work. With no GPS in the *Plywood Princess* (or live well, or trolling motor), he'll have to make it all work the old-fashioned way. He does have a few sweet rod holders mounted, though.

Gus navigates into a slow no-wake area under a bridge, meeting a huge yacht heading in the same direction. He yields to the big boat, and slips in behind to approach the narrow channel, single file. About six bikini-clad girls, tan, and sipping beverages are in the back of the big boat, now just a few feet away. The cursive script on the back of the boat is *C Angel*, and it probably should be on a "sea" and not on a lake. It's big—over 40 feet!

Doogie stares, well...all three boys stare, but Doogie has a way of staring more loudly.

Gus wishes he could snap his fingers or fly through a chimney and they'd transport to their fishing spot. He's been in the *Plywood Princess* next to big yachts before. There's no way this is going to go the way Doogie thinks. "Hey girls. Beautiful day," Doogie flirts.

"What? Did you say something?" They know he did, and they probably heard him, too.

"I just said, 'it sure is a beautiful day today', don't you think?"

"Oh." One girl looks at the others, imploring if she should have heard that, or answer.

"That sure is a nice boat you've got there." The music pulses loudly from the party boat, only a few feet ahead.

"Doogie, knock it off," Gus begs, just above a whisper. "We're in the freaking *Plywood Princess*, and they are in a million-dollar boat. Okay? Let it go."

"What?" Doogie feigns the injured party.

"Just ignore them."

"I can't ignore them. They're g-o-r-g-e-o-u-s, or haven't you noticed?"

"I noticed, from the *Plywood Princess*. We're not exactly in my dad's Ranger, are we?"

"Oh. I didn't think of that."

Gus is certain the girls are all laughing at his little orange aluminum fishing boat. When he first got it, he was so proud. But enough snide comments from bigger, nicer boats on the lake over the last two summers have dampened Gus' enthusiasm for his rig.

They reach the end of the slow no-wake channel and *C Angel* turns and powers up, kicking up a wake that could capsize the boys without Gus' careful maneuvers to quarter-cut them. No worries. Gus handles his little craft like a proud captain. Check that. Maybe not all that proud. Skilled.

"Gus?" Doogie asks, as the little boat settles from the huge rockers. "What does the C stand for in your name?" Apparently the *C Angel* has reminded Doogie of an incident from class recently, and the bus ride home with Matt Driver.

They motor along, slowly. There's no place to go. Three boys in the boat and one of them doesn't want to talk about it. They are friends and Doogie asked a reasonable question. He's not making fun, or picking a fight, he's just asking. In Gus' perfect world it just wouldn't come up.

Thinking, stalling, the question hangs in the silence for a moment. A long moment. "I have a legal first name that starts with a C." Gus wonders if this will be enough. Sensing it isn't, he goes on. "Gustav is my full middle name, everybody just calls me Gus, that's all."

"Doogie and I were talking that we should know what it is, Gus. We're your best friends for heaven's sake."

"I know," Gus replies, feeling a little bad."But I don't like it, it's kind of embarrassing."

"Embarassing?" Asher gets red in the face, his voice cracks as the volume goes up. "How about MY name, Gus? Asher?! Sheesh, you know darn well what people do to my name and how they tease me." Asher looks hard at Gus, and then away.

"I'm sorry, I never thought your name was bad. It's just... unusual."

"Try that argument the next time Matt Driver calls me ash hole, which happens pretty regularly."

Gus realizes that Asher probably does have a valid beef about his name. People, especially rude and mean people, can use anything to tease. Too tall. Too short. Too this, too that. "I'm sorry, Asher. I guess you're right. But you of all people should understand that I don't want my first name known by everybody. A first initial works for F. Scott Fitzgerald or J. Edgar Hoover. Okay?"

An uneasy silence falls across the boat. Doogie and Asher exchange a look, disappointed that their friend doesn't trust them enough with his secret. Gus looks up at the fancy mansions along the shoreline with their big, expensive yachts at the docks. He should be grateful for his little orange aluminum boat, but he's not. He wants more: faster, bigger, more. He avoids glancing the direction of his friends, and wishes this conversation never happened.

# Chapter 6

That night, Gus approaches his dad about an idea, while Jake is hauling sand.

"I was thinking, Dad." Money has been on Gus' mind a lot since yesterday. "Maybe we could shave off some of our expenses for the fishing tournament in September. I have a couple of ideas."

"Okay, what are you thinking?"

"Well, you said the total package would include hotel, eating out, gas, bait and entry fee, right?"

"Right."

"What if we borrowed Grandpa Bud's RV so we didn't have any hotel expense, and we brought our own food along so we didn't have to eat out in restaurants? That would save us some money."

"I guess it would, a little." Jim's excited to fish a tournament with his son, and Gus couldn't be happier to have a pro-level tournament in his near future. He's been counting down the days until he's eligible. "But it wouldn't save much. The RV is pretty bad in gas mileage. We'd drop almost as much on gas as motel rooms. They aren't very expensive in Webster, South Dakota, Gus."

"I suppose. But what about eating at restaurants?"

"True, we'd save some money with our own food. Maybe we could bring some stuff already made up, like sloppy joe's or something. I'm not much of a cook, you know."

"Or we could grill hamburgers or make hobo pies. That's easy. And the RV is really fun to stay in."

"I'll ask Grandpa."

"Thanks, Dad."

"No problem, Gus. Why are you thinking about this September tournament now?"

"I'm worried with the hours at Dr. Cavendish's house, I won't have my half covered."

"Bummer having to work for a living, eh?"

"Yeah, big time."

The birds call for Gus to get up and come outside the next morning. It is a beautiful day, but Gus sleeps in until eight, ignoring their invitation. It is the first day without school after all. Then he gets up and turns on his computer, launches a quick MapQuest of Webster, South Dakota to get an idea of Waubay Lake's geography. This way he knows what's around it, and how far it is from home. Then he bings Waubay Lake to see what else he can find. There's plenty. Maps that show the water levels, and how it has changed over the years. Waubay is a lake that doubled in size in the 1990's. Gus learns a lot about what the bottom is like, and where there's structure, by looking at the maps of the terrain before it flooded.

He reads fishing reports from local guys about the quality of the fish and a lot of the common techniques. Gus absorbs all this information. Oops. It's 9:15 and more than an hour has slipped by. He runs to the kitchen and puts down two pieces of toast, smears them with peanut butter when they pop. He snarfs it all down in a hurry, with a full glass chug of orange juice. Time to get to work, he grabs a pair of work gloves from the garage and walks three doors down.

"Good morning, Mrs. C." Gus is checking in for his first day on the job. "Ready for work, today. Do you want me to report in to you at the house before I get started each day? Or just get started?"

"This is good, Gus," Mickey replies. "Stop by so I know when you arrive, and we can chat about your assignments for the day. And stop by when you're leaving, so I know that, too. Okay?"

"Yes, ma'am. What's the plan?"

Mrs. C gives Gus the run down on what to do and in what order. He gets at it. Promptly at noon he stops by to let her know that he's done for the day, unless there's anything else she wants done, hoping that she'll change her mind on 'full-stop' at noon.

"Let's take a look at what you did this morning," Mickey replies as she slips on her sandals, lined up neatly by the front door. "A little quality control, Gus."

"Yes, ma'am." They walk to the beach where Gus was instructed to clean up weeds, dead fish, tree branches and such that accumulate.

"Wow. This looks great."

"Good, I'm glad you like it."

"No Gus, I love it. It looks really great. It reminds me of a beachfront hotel in the Florida Keys. They had their beach raked perfectly every day—just like this."

Gus smiles, thankful that his hard work and attention to detail is appreciated by his new boss.

"How did you clean up this section?" Mrs. C is below a big willow tree. There used to be tree roots sticking up above the sand, now it's smooth and clean.

"Oh, I trimmed the roots back a little bit. They'll still get their water below the surface."

"How'd you do that?"

"A saw."

"Really? Where did you find it?"

"In the garage, next to the tools you told me to use. You want to see the landscape rocks that I started to clean? I'm not done yet, I'll need more days unless you want me to stay longer today." The two walk over to the side of the house with landscape rock behind a black rubber edging. One section looks clean and brand new. The other sections, and there a lot of them, look dirty, with tree debris everywhere and clumps of dirt mixed on top the rocks.

"This looks great, Gus. I'm very happy with your work."

"Thanks, ma'am. You want me to stay a little longer?"

"No, I have some painting to do this afternoon, and I simply must have peace and quiet while I'm working. But I'll see you back tomorrow morning. 9:30."

"Yes ma'am. See you tomorrow." Happy with the enthusiasm

from his new boss, but disappointed that she's not going to budge on the 9:30 to noon work day—every other week no less. Maybe he can get the off weeks worked in, he'll see how that looks later in the summer. The good part of Mrs. C's schedule is that it leaves plenty of time to play and fish. Bad part is the hours rack up slowly, and that means the bank account won't be where he needs it to be by September.

# Chapter 7

That night, Annie and Pops organize a fish fry with the walleyes that Gus caught yesterday with Asher and Doogie. They had a productive day on Crystal Bay with leech-tipped Lindy rigs. Did their job.

"Oil's ready." Pops has the fryer set up on the deck.

"Okay, here's the stuff." Annie hands him the clean fillets and the egg wash and seasoned coating. Pops will man the fryer with a big tongs. Everyone is seated around the patio table, enjoying a beautiful evening by the lake, with a nice breeze blowing off the water so it isn't too hot.

The patio table is set with the summer plates and cups for outside use. As the first fillets come out of the oil, Dad leads grace while they cool and drain on a bed of paper towels. They all dig in. Pops puts the next batch into the oil and sits down to eat his meal, too.

"Good progress on the sand pile, Jake." Jim smiles when it says it. He and Annie aren't the type to scream and yell if their kids screw up, but that doesn't mean there won't be consequences.

"Yeah. About halfway I guess," Jake laments.

"You'll get it done."

"Yeah, I will. But I gotta work at Rockvam tomorrow, too. So it might take a few days."

"No problem Jakey-boy," Pops jumps in. "The days are long this time of year. It's not dark until ten o'clock."

"True that."

Annie and Jim exchange a look, and the conversation lulls for a moment. A long moment. Gus picks up on it and asks, "What's going on?"

"Well…" Jim mutters. There's that look again between the two of them.

"Go ahead, Jim. Tell them," Annie suggests.

"Okay, there's something we want to talk about tonight."

Gus and Jake exchange a look, and Jake turns pale. He's worried there's more punishment for his speeding ticket, as if 22 tons of sand isn't enough.

"Jake wasn't really even speeding Dad, I told you that." Gus tries to help.

"No, that's not it." There's a pause, a l-o-n-g pause. Then finally: "We're going to have another baby."

Silence.

More silence, looks exchange between the three guys that are caught off-guard with the news. So this is what shock looks like.

"Aren't you guys excited?" Dad scans the faces of his three comrades, and the disappointment creeps into his face. The answer is obvious. No they are not excited. "Don't you want to say congratulations or something?"

Jim looks over at Annie, who doesn't look amused at all. In fact, she looks like she's about to cry. "It's good news boys, come on!" she forces a smile as she says it. "I may have been a little bit surprised, too, at first. But we're very happy and very lucky. You're going to have a sister."

A sister? Oh boy.

"Right as rain, that's what!" Pops finally finds his voice. "Congratulations, Annie. Can't wait to have a wee-high keiki girl in the family."

The two boys exchange a look. Jake's look says—OMG can you believe it and Gus's look back says—What will it be like with a baby around here? They both shake their heads in answer.

"I guess I should say congratulations," says Jake. "But I'm in shock. I didn't know this was coming. I mean, a baby? It's a bit embarrassing. What will my friends say?"

"Oh good grief, Jake." Dad sounds a little irritated. "Families have babies. It happens."

"But I'm 16 years old," Jake whines. "When is the baby due? I'll be almost 17 years old!"

"The baby's due in the fall—October," says Mom. "You have time to get used to it."

"What will it be like having a baby?" Gus asks. Jake gives Gus a look that calls him a dweeb without saying it out loud. "Wait. I didn't mean *that*. I mean, will you still work after you have the baby or will you stay home to take care of it—er, her."

Mom laughs and Gus feels better. He always like it when his mom laughs. "Gus, no worries. I'll take a leave from work so that I can be home for a few months and then we'll either get a nanny or arrange for childcare. The timing is actually pretty good, the season will be over so it should quiet down during the off-season."

"Perfectamundo," offers Pops. "How ya been feelin' Annie?"

Gus' mind races through 100 different things as the conversation with the family continues around him. What room will she get? Will they have to move bedrooms? Will she cry a lot at night or during the day? When will she walk and talk? Can they still take vacations and go fun places? Does Gus have to take care of her? Change dirty diapers? Yikes. Gus doesn't ask any of them—yet.

Maybe she'll be fun and cute. Maybe she'll want Gus to teach her how to fish. Maybe she won't cry and maybe she'll laugh and think she has two awesome big brothers.

"Wow. I'm gonna be a big brother." Gus jumps back into the conversation. "I've always been the little brother. Things are changing."

"Yes, they are, son," replies Dad.

"This won't affect our tournament on Waubay in September, will it, Dad?"

Dad looks over at Annie. "No, I don't think so."

"Pinky promise?" Gus wants to lock his dad into that one.

"I can't pinky promise that, Gus," Dad replies as he shakes his head. "There are some things in life that we just don't control. Exactly when a baby arrives is one of them." Sheesh. Gus' stomach does a flip and a lurch. Now the tournament he is so excited about is in jeopardy.

Later, exhausted from a long day, Gus looks up at the ceiling in his room, lying in bed. Neon-glo stars, stuck to the drywall with tape, illuminate his home-made constellation—and faraway thoughts. He can't stop thinking about a baby in the family. How will everything change? Will he like the changes or hate them? He'll be mad if he can't fish that tournament in September, especially after all the hard work to raise money. What difference does it make what he thinks? He can't stop it.

Then he realizes that his mom could stop it—and isn't. What if she was the type that didn't like surprises? What if he was a surprise back before he was born? Maybe he was. Good thing that brothers (that don't want to rock their world with a baby) don't get to decide, or Jake might not have wanted Gus in the family picture. Lots to think about.

*Dear God,*

*I got some big news in our family tonight about a new baby. Do you already know that? I think you do because you are God and you know everything—even before it happens. You knew about me before I was born. I guess that means that you know about this baby sister. Do you love her already? I think I'm supposed to love her, but I don't know just yet. Help me to love this new baby and to be a good brother. Thank you for summer vacation, for nice walleyes that we had for dinner tonight and for my summer job and my family. Help Jake move all the sand that he needs to move and help Mom and Dad with this new baby, and please keep Pops healthy. Be with Zach and Riley with their wedding coming up, too. And if it's not too much trouble, I still need to make some more money this summer. I'm gonna need a little help.*

*Amen.*

# Chapter 8

"Okay, see you tomorrow night." Jake says goodbye to Mom as she drops him off at Rockvam on her way downtown. He'll drive to Wisconsin to meet up with the Roberts side of the family after he gets off work at five o'clock on Saturday. That should put him in about nine o'clock.

Jim has two sisters that live in Wisconsin, and one has a son that is graduating from high school and a big grad party is planned for Sunday. Deuce is two years older than Jake, the oldest grandchild on that side of the family. That's his nickname, and everybody uses it.

The sisters are twins, identical twins. Some of the time Jake and Gus can tell them apart, but sometimes it can be really tricky and the sisters just laugh when someone gets it wrong. So they're both "Aunt Sis" or even simply "Sis" to their nieces and nephews, minimizing the need to remember which one is Carla and which one is Connie. Too complicated.

"Have a good day at work, and drive carefully. Keep an eye on Pops for me, and feed Quick." Mom reminds Jake as he slams the door of her car.

Quick is the family's yellow Labrador retriever. At ten years old, Dad worries that Quick's now a little too old for hunting. Last year after pheasant hunting, he could hardly walk for a week. Poor Quick. He's not so quick anymore. If Quick were younger, it would be fun to take him to Wisconsin. He used to love to run with Aunt Sis' horses. But now it's easier for him to stay home with Pops, and Pops doesn't mind a break with a quiet house for a change. It'll be crazy in Wisconsin with all of Dad's family around.

After everyone is off to work on Friday morning, Gus arrives for his last morning of the week at Dr. and Mrs. C's house. Promptly at the designated time, Gus knocks on her door to let her know that he's reporting for duty.

"Oh hi, Gus. Is it 9:30 already?"

"Yes, ma'am, it is. I'm here now and will hopefully finish up the landscape rock project today."

"That's great, Gus. What you've done looks great. I showed it to Doc last night when he got home and he was very happy. How are you getting those rocks so clean?"

"I made a sieve with some old window screens that you had in your garage. I put the rocks on the screen, hose them down and then let them accumulate and dry off in the wheelbarrow, until I'm ready to dump a clean load back on the spot."

"It looks great."

"Are you sure you don't want me to work next week? I know you have the landscape company next week, but I could still do some other projects." Gus crosses his fingers behind his back while he asks.

"No, I don't think so. You've done a great job, Gus. But I like the work the landscape company does, too, and I don't want to lose them either. I'll see you a week from Monday at 9:30."

"Okay."

"Stop back at noon and I'll pay you for the week."

"Yes, ma'am. Thank you."

Gus gets busy on shoveling, cleaning, and dumping landscape rock. Lots of landscape rock. Wheelbarrows and wheelbarrows full of landscape rock. At noon he gets paid from Mrs. C and puts it in a safe spot in his room, until he can take it to the bank. A little after three o'clock the family hits the road, anxious for dinner with the Roberts clan.

Jim is lucky with his line of work, he can usually make his own schedule and fits photo shoots around what the family needs. But Annie's job is a little more demanding, and it can be tricky. It's hard to get her away from the office, but it is even harder to get her away from the work. People still call all the time. The first hour of the drive is filled with phone calls, mostly about the All-Star game coming up next month. It's in Washington D.C. and there are lots of details and promotional events with clients around the event.

"Dad, maybe we should go along for the All-Star game next month."

"I can't Gus, the I-CAST show is in Las Vegas the same week. I had thought about it, but they almost always fall on the same week." I-CAST is the trade show for the sportfishing industry.

"What do you have to do at I-CAST?"

"It's a big show, Gus, and almost all of my fishing clients exhibit there. I can see all of them within a few days, and it is always good to stay in touch and keep the network alive and well."

"Will you take any pictures or just go to meetings?"

"I'll take photos, Gus. Pitchers are for baseball and pictures are paintings that hang on the wall. Photography is what I do."

"Sorry, forgot." Gus' dad is a little touchy about calling it 'taking pictures.'

"And yes, I'll still take some photos while I'm there. But mostly I'll make sure that I have catalogs, ads, magazine covers and other business on deck for the next year. Maybe a few TV shows for video. We'll have another mouth to feed soon." Dad chuckles as he says it.

"Will you see any pro fishermen there?"

"Absolutely, a lot of them." Jim moves the windshield wipers to full blast. The rain is really come down now.

"Like who?"

Jim rattles off a dozen names like Kevin VanDam, Mike Iaconelli, Larry Nixon, Jay Yelas, Johnnie Candle, Tommy Skarlis, Ted Takasaki and Greg Yarbrough—just to name a few.

Gus has met Tommy Skarlis and Ted Takasaki from the list his dad mentions. Maybe it would be fun to go to I-CAST with him.

"How about you get Pops to go along to the All-Star game in July?" Annie is finally off the phone. Her cell phone battery is probably shot by now.

"That would be fun, Gus. Ask Pops if he wants to go with you." Jim thinks it is a good idea.

"Hmm. A city full of pro baseball players or a city full of pro fishermen. Dilemma."

Annie laughs out loud. "Only you, Gus, would say that. Only you."

They get to Wisconsin, just in time for chicken on the grill. Grandpa Bud and Grandma Dee arrived earlier in the morning with their RV. Gus is excited to see his cousin, Colton, who is only a few weeks younger than Gus. Zach and Riley, who's wedding is now just a month away, are there. Everyone but Jake, and he'll drive over tomorrow night.

"Hey, Colton!"

"Hey, Gus!" The cousins exchange hugs. They're a huggy kind of family. All the cousins and aunts and uncles stop their conversations to welcome the last group to arrive for the weekend.

Deuce raps Gus on the head, lightly. "Hey, little dude, where's your big brother?"

"He's coming tomorrow night. He has to work tomorrow 'til five."

Deuce noogies Colton hard.

"Dough-ent," Colton replies with a whine. Deuce laughs at him and walks away. The Wisconsin cousins can turn a one syllable word like don't into two syllables. How do they do that?

"Sorry we're late," Annie owns the delay in the schedule. "I couldn't get out of the office very early today."

"That's okay, we're glad you're here now." Aunt Sis exclaims, just don't ask which Aunt Sis it is.

Word has gotten out to the family that a baby girl is on the way for Jim and Annie, and there's lots of commotion talking about babies, with congratulations and high pitched voices in a buzz. Aunt Sis has a one-year-old girl, Colton's youngest sister, Rachael. Colton and Gus go through the buffet line for food and take theirs downstairs to the family room.

"So, you're going to have a baby sister, eh?" Colton asks Gus.

They aren't in the U.P. of Michigan, but sometimes it sounds like it.

"Yeah, October."

"A World Series baby. Let's hope the Twins aren't in it this year."

"What? How can you say that?!" Gus' mouth is wide open, betrayal from his cousin, rocking his world. They are both big Twins fan. Even though the cousins live in Wisconsin, most of them are Minnesota fans in football and baseball.

"Your mom won't be able to deal with her team in the World Series and have a baby at the same time, can she?"

Gus hadn't thought of that. He was just thinking about his tournament in September and forgot that autumn could be a really hard time for his mom to deliver a baby. "We're off to a good start this year, we definitely should be in the playoffs. World Series would be s-w-e-e-t. We're in first place, but Detroit is only one game back and the White Sox are only three games back. There's a lot of season left."

"I know. You're so lucky. Will you get tickets if they get into the playoffs."

"Yeah, I guess so. To some of the games anyway."

"I hate you, Gus." Colton says with a smile and a shake of his head, signaling subconsciously, that he doesn't really mean it.

Gus just smiles at his cousin that is a great friend. Not all cousins are, but it's great when it works out that way. "You got everything ready?"

"Nope, too wet. We'll have to wait until tomorrow."

"Darn."

"Tell me something I don't know." The lightning strikes like an exclamation point, lighting up the sky, and the crack of thunder rattles the glass in the walkout basement patio doors. It's a doozie of a storm. Good night to stay in.

# Chapter 9

The next morning the boys are up early, the only other ones up are Aunt Sis and little Rachael. The boys find them in the kitchen as they grab a bite to eat. Babies. Something new for Gus to think about.

"Good morning, boys." Aunt Sis feeds little Rachael in a high chair.

"Morning Mom. Morning peanut." Rachael's eyes brighten with glee when she sees her big brother. He comes over and steals a bite of Cheerios from her out-stretched hand.

"Morning." Gus takes it all in. He hadn't really paid much attention to Rachael before.

"What're you boys up to this morning? Let me guess—fishing?"

"How did ya know?"

"What else would have you up so early on a Saturday morning in June." Sis laughs, and spoons some cut-up scrambled egg onto Rachael's tray.

"We're going to set up the tent out in Beautiful World. Sleepin' there tonight, Mom."

"Okay. Good thing the storm blew through last night. Should give you a nice night out there." Gus comes a little closer to Rachael, and she lights up with two boys to entertain with her high chair antics. He smiles at her and she giggles back. "So you're getting a little sister, too, Gus? Kind of exciting."

"Yeah. Getting used to the idea I guess."

"We'll see you later, eh?" Colton grabs a mitt full of granola bars and two apples and motions for Gus to keep moving.

The boys walk down to the barn to locate two of the ATVs, watched the last 100 yards by the herd of black and white Friesian horses. Gus takes a deep breath, and fills his lungs with the smell of the farm, loving it. Even the bad smells are good smells to him, signaling life outdoors in a natural world.

Gus and Colton load up the tent, and a tarp for the ground under the tent floor, strapping it to the back with rubber tie-downs. Fishing gear is not forgotten and placed carefully on the top, secure under the straps. Not only will they be fishing this morning but they need to set up their tent for camping in Beautiful World tonight.

"Let's take the long route this morning." Colton and his older brother and cousins have built up dozens of trails that meander through their 130 acres.

"Okay, but that's less time for fishing." Gus is always mindful of keeping his line wet, and lives by the mantra that you can't catch anything if your line isn't wet, no matter what color your lure is.

"True that."

"How about the route that you lose your stomach? And we take it really fast?" One of the paths has hills that roll and if you catch it at the right speed your stomach will lurch with the fight of gravity.

"Perfect. See you at Beautiful World."

Beautiful World is a special place for Colton and all the cousins. It is a clearing that the uncles created, nestled right up against a wide spot on Junebug Creek. A big fire pit has been dug, with cords of wood stacked up all around. Some big tree logs form benches around the campfire. And they don't have to share it with anyone. It's on their own land and no one else goes back there, a quiet getaway tucked into the woods, several miles from the house and barn.

Colton leads the way with a heavy hand on the throttle. He's been ATVing his whole life and lives just on the edge of scary when he drives. Gus has to work hard to keep up with him, only four-wheeling a few times a year, not every week. They fly across the top of the hillcrest, and through muddy puddles at each low point, throwing up debris at whatever, or whoever, is behind them.

There are five rolling hills and each time the boys crest the top at a blazing speed, what they know is coming still delights when it arrives—the tummy tickle.

Soon they slow as they move away from the open land and into the woods. The trail has sharp twists and turns and a few steep climbs and sharp drops as they make their way back. When they arrive and turn off the motors, their bodies still tingle with the hum of the engine from underneath. It takes a few moments to wear off and the boys drink in the stillness and quiet, knowing this is their place for the next two days. Neither boy breaks the silence for a long time with any words. They relax and enjoy it, together.

Eventually, they unload their gear and the magic is broken. Gus is covered in mud.

"Fishing first?" You-know-who wants to get his line wet, happy that his St. Croix spinning rod survived four-wheeling.

"Roger that."

"Besides, that will give the ground a little more time to dry out after the rain last night." The flat area for the tent is hard clay with more weeds than grass, but an hour or two of sunshine will probably do it good.

"And you can dry off too, Gus." Colton watches as Gus washes off some of the mud encrusted from the run. "Is that your new rod?"

"Yup. Got it for Christmas. St. Croix."

"S-w-e-e-t."

"It is. We can switch for awhile if you want. I'd like to try your fly rod anyway."

"Sure."

Colton enjoys fly fishing on the creek, and has a nice set up from Shakespeare. It's nothing too fancy, but it gets the job done. Probably the right choice over an expensive fly rod, since the four-wheeling ride is pretty rough travel to and from.

The boys enjoy the time at the creek, not needing conversation to have fun. When you both enjoy what you're doing, extra words aren't always necessary. Fishing with different techniques, both use hair jigs to entice the trout out of the stream. It works. However, today the boys decide to make it a catch-and-release day. Colton snaps photos of each catch, though, with his iPhone, proof of their accomplished morning on the water.

Gus is just a little jealous. He doesn't have any cell phone yet, let alone an iPhone. Heck, even Jake just got a cell phone after he got his driver's license, since Mom didn't want him driving without a way to call for help if there's trouble.

After they have their fun on the water, they set up the tent and make more trips back to the house for stuff like sleeping bags, pillows, hobo pie irons and snacks; reconnecting with civilization just long enough to re-stock on food and gasoline, not to mention the fondness for real bathrooms with toilet paper—a beautiful thing.

# Chapter 10

"What time do we need to be back?" Gus hikes through the woods, hunting up morel mushrooms with Colton. The Roberts family treasures morels. Fried up they are a tasty treat.

"I don't know. I don't think they care."

"Really? I think my folks will care."

"I have my cell phone, if they want us, they'll call. Besides, the party isn't until tomorrow. Today's a lazy day."

"Didn't think of that. But you know how they get, especially when it's close to meal time." Gus spots the crisscross diamond shape bark of an ash tree and makes a widening search in a circle around the tree. He spots a nice grouping of yellow morels and adds them to his meshy onion bag.

"True that. How about I call them?"

"Good diarrhea." Oops. Gus cringes. Pops says that for good idea sometimes, it can be a little contagious. "Pops says it for good idea. Sorry."

Colton chuckles and proceeds to dial HOME on his contact list. It rings and rings and no one answers. "Hmm. No answer."

"Let's check it out."

"Yeah, let's take what we have for morels in, and see what's up. Can't be that no one is home, can it?"

"Hard to believe."

The two use the opportunity as an excuse to ride hard and fast. As they round the horse pasture they see most all of the family at the horse fence and slow w-a-y down. All the horses are congregated, excited for a little attention.

"Hi," Colton calls to his mom, the biggest horse lover of them all, careful not to go too fast and get yelled at if they spook the horses.

"Hi, boys," Carla replies with a big grin. "Just showing everybody my new babies." Carla has two mares that foaled this spring, and she loves having foals in the herd.

"We were wondering about dinner?"

"Imagine that, hungry boys." Jim walks over by Gus. Zach and Riley follow. It is a beautiful summer evening and everyone is enjoying being outside on these long days.

"I think we're all going to the Corner Bar for prime rib tonight," Zach chimes in. "No urchins, though."

"Well, I think maybe Rachael is going with us," Riley adds.

"She is not an urchin…yet." Zach laughs.

"What are we, chopped liver?" Colton protests, knowing how good the steaks are at the Corner Bar.

"Yeah, sorry guys." Aunt Sis says the word sorry, but doesn't look it. "Deuce is inside with a bunch of his friends, and they had a pile of pizzas delivered."

"Pizza? Let's go." The two boys head to the house in search of hot pizza, and find it downstairs in the family room, following the noise. Deuce is hanging with a lot of his friends, playing pool and listening to music. The pizzas are on a table with cheesy bread. Jackpot.

"Grab some pizza," Colton suggests. He doesn't have to say it twice.

"Mmm. Good," Gus offers between bites, scanning the room. There are a lot of Deuce's friends over—a lot of girls. In fact, there are more girls than boys at this party.

"Hey, if it isn't Pete and Repeat," Deuce hollers when he sees Gus and Colton snarf down pizza. "Are you going to chip in to buy some of that pizza, dweebs?"

"Like you paid a penny for this pizza, Deuce," snaps Colton, irritated his brother's giving him a hard time in front of all his friends, especially all these girls. "I know Mom or Dad bought the pizzas anyways, not you."

"Mr. Know-It-All, eh?" retorts Deuce. "I have an idea. How would you like to make 20 bucks, little bro?" He asks in a sweet voice. Too sweet. Something's up.

"Twenty bucks?" Gus wonders out loud. "Holy cow." Twenty bucks is a lot of money. What is he up to?

"Sure," says Colton with a little bit of swagger. "Name your bet!"

"It isn't a bet, peon," Deuce says loudly. Some of the girls walk over by the pizza table to find out what's going on. "Just a simple thing to do."

"All right, what is it?" asks Colton.

Deuce picks up the Parmesan cheese shaker and the chili pepper shakers next to the pizza, one in each hand. "Snort a handful of this up your nose!" All the girls laugh as Deuce holds up the peppers and puts down the cheese shaker. Uh-oh. Snort chili peppers up your nose?

Colton looks at Gus with a look that says—I can't back down from my brother now, and Gus gives Colton a look back that says— Twenty bucks is a lot of money. Then one of the girls says, "Twenty dollars is a lot of money," almost like she was reading Gus' mind. She looks at Colton with a look that says—Do it.

"Show me the 20 bucks," Colton says to Deuce. Obviously, Colton doesn't trust him.

"No problem, dweeb." He pulls a crisp 20 dollar bill from his pocket and waves it around. The girls giggle. Everyone watches as Deuce shakes out the peppers into the palm of Colton's hand.

Colton looks closely, studying the peppers and maybe willing them to disappear. Deuce doesn't say a word, just stares his little brother down. But all Deuce's friends shout: "Do it! Do it! Do it!"

He does it. Snort. A handful of chili peppers right up his nose.

Of course it hurts, it has to hurt. Poor Colton. Tears pool in his eyes—not because he's crying, but because those peppers have got to be hot inside his sinuses. Yikes. Gus has a sympathy taste in his own nose and looks sadly at his cousin.

Deuce and all his friends laugh and pat Colton on the back, watching intently as he turns from red to white and back to red again. One girl, Ashley, according to her sweatshirt, comes over and gives him a big kiss on his cheek. Colton looks horrible, like he can't even breathe (poor guy) and can't believe a pretty girl kissed him while he's feeling so miserable. "You're very brave," Ashley tells him quietly, so close her lips touch his ear. "And 20 dollars richer." She stands so close to him that he can feel his face hot and red, hers cool and calm. "Go get your cash," she prompts him, with a whisper.

Colton walks over to his brother with his hand out. "No problem little bro," says Deuce through his laughter, as he hands over the money. "That was definitely 20 dollars worth of entertainment." He laughs and so do all his friends.

"You know, Colt," says Deuce a little too sweetly, as he walks over to the sink in the bar area. "It might feel a lot better for you if you come rinse that out with some fresh clean water, buddy."

Oh no. Don't do it. Gus thinks it but his words are stuck inside, standing so close to Ashley. But it's too late. Colton steps over to the sink and turns on the tap. He lets some water pool into his cupped hand and snorts it up into his nose to clear out the peppers. Only problem is, now he has water up his nose. That has to be just as bad as the peppers.

Deuce laughs again and so do all his friends. "Colton, you are so stupid!"

Gus knows they need to leave and pulls Colton up the stairs, the sound of laughter drifting below as they climb to the main floor. In the kitchen, Colton steadies himself while Gus packs food to take to the tent. They can't wait to get out of the house.

The boys speed as fast as they can with the four-wheelers back to Beautiful World. They'll have the campsite to themselves tonight and plenty of food and water.

"How you doing?" Gus asks as they lay out the kindling for the fire and settle the stuff inside the tent.

"I'm fine," Colton says, a little bit embarrassed and glad the effects of the chili peppers are diminishing. "Deuce can be such a jerk sometimes."

Gus doesn't have a brother that's a jerk, so he can't relate. To Gus it would be like living with Matt Driver and that would be horrible. Jake and Gus get along okay—most of the time. Gus knew that Colton got picked on by his older brother but he's seen it first-hand now. "It would drive me crazy," Gus says. "But Ashley was right, man. You're 20 dollars richer, and you took it from Deuce!" Gus offers a high five and Colton breaks a smile and laughs.

"Dude, she kissed me!" says Colton exuberantly. "Did you see that?"

"Boy did I. She's a beautiful girl and she kissed you, Colton. Lucky duck."

Little did the boys know that their fun would take a completely different turn later that night. Deuce and company have a few more ideas for mischief up their sleeves.

# Chapter 11

Colton and Gus build an amazing fire—without cheating. Only losers need gasoline to build a fire. Not these two. But there is a red gas can nearby in case the four-wheelers run out in the woods.

They lay out the kindling on the bottom of the fire pit and then position long, dry sticks into a tepee shape to let the air through. Once they light the dried leaves the kindling takes off. As soon as the tepee part is on fire and drops down to the bottom, they add the larger logs that will burn with a lot of heat, and for a long time. It is a beautiful fire in Beautiful World. Gus enjoys the warmth while Colton walks away for awhile, closer to the creek. A few minutes alone is maybe what Colton is looking for, and Gus gives it to him. Colton casts his fly rod a few times to relieve some tension. Then leans it up against a tree by the shoreline when he's done. He walks back to the fire as Gus grabs the hobo pie irons. "What are you doin', Gus? We don't have stuff for hobo pies."

"I have an idea. Check this." Gus puts Grandma Dee's chocolate chip cookies inside the pie iron and then puts the iron in the campfire. A minute later they open the pie iron to discover melty chocolate chip cookies like they just came out of the oven, only a little bit squished.

"Awesome." Colton enjoys the gooey mess, too. They eat every single cookie that they brought.

"Three-in-a-row?" Gus asks Colton. Three-in-a-row is a game the family plays. Well, Gus enjoys it immensely, and the rest of the family members play along. Each asks the other three questions to answer about vocabulary words. They can be for a specific group name, gender name or baby name for animals, birds or insects.

"Sure, you want to go first?" replies Colton.

"No way, you go first," Gus answers with a smile. "You're the man of the hour tonight. I think you're acting President of the Studly Brotherhood tonight." They laugh. Uncle Zach started the Studly Brotherhood and all the guys are members. It's supposed to help all of the brothers and cousins get along, and come to each other's rescue if you ever need it.

"Okay, the theme is insects," launches Colton. "Cockroaches?"

"That's a good one, Colt," Gus answers. "You're much better at this game than Jake. He asks easy ones all the time. Intrusion. An intrusion of cockroaches."

"Hey, when I know you're gonna visit, I get prepared." Colton smiles. "Okay, gnats?"

"A cloud of gnats."

"Darn. I thought I'd get you on that one. You're good. Two out of three, Gus. Let's see, you probably know this one. Mosquitoes?" Very timely, they're applying bug spray because the mosquitoes are thick as thieves in the woods.

"Hmm. Mosquitoes?" Gus isn't sure. He can't believe he hasn't learned this one and that it hasn't ever come up before. "Sheesh, Colt, I don't know. Swarm?" He doesn't sound very confident, and Colton knows it.

Colton makes the sound of a game show buzzer going off—ERRR! "Well...I guess any insect is a swarm to some degree. But a swarm of mosquitoes is technically a scourge. So I'll give you half a point."

"Scourge. Cool. Glad I learned something new today. My turn?"

"Fire away, no pun intended." They are hanging by their campfire in Beautiful World, enjoying life, roasting hot dogs.

"The theme is birds," Gus says with a mouthful as he takes his turn. "Woodpeckers?" Gus learned this one from Pops a couple of weeks ago. It's a good one.

"Flock," Colton answers.

"Half a point. Flock fits for any group of birds, kind of like swarm for insects. The unique group name for woodpeckers is descent."

"Really?" asks Colton. "Descent?"

"Yup. That's a doozie, isn't it?"

"Sure is."

"Next—owls?"

"I believe a group of owls," Colton says in a stuffy British accent. "Is called a parliament, young man." They both laugh. He nailed it.

"Good one, Colt. You're a lot better at this game now than you were last summer. "Last one—ravens?"

"Oh darn it," Colton moans. "And just after you told me I'm getting better at this game. I don't know, Gus. What is a group of ravens called?"

"An unkindness of ravens. Cool?"

"Yeah, that's a good one, too. An unkindness of ravens." Colton repeats it, to anchor the new word in his memory.

They spend the rest of the evening talking about fishing and baseball and the Stanley Cup Finals, fun stuff that they both like. Eventually the fire gets puny and they get cold. Colton's iPhone vibrates with a text message from his mom, checking in that he and Gus are all right in Beautiful World. He replies back that everything is fine and they are about to turn in for sleep.

As they douse the fire and head to the tent, Colton asks Gus, "So, are you excited about a baby in your family?"

"To be honest, I wasn't at first. But I think I'm getting used to the idea."

"It'll be all right."

"You would know, having a baby sister already."

"She's the best, I really love the little peanut."

"I can see that when I'm with you. That's great. I don't quite feel it yet."

"Don't worry about it, you will. It's just someone new into the family. Like Riley marrying Zach. We always have enough love for another one, right?"

"I hadn't thought of it that way. Good point."

After they remove the gummie bears that Zach (probably) put at the bottom of their sleeping bags, they settle in with the lantern light off and tell stories. There are two rules of storytelling. Rule number one is all stories must be whispered. Rule number two is it must be made up as you go, the teller leaves a pause and the listener (or listeners) jump in with some new twist that you have to incorporate into the story. Gus starts because he's older, a few weeks anyway.

"Once upon a time there was an old man and his pet...," Gus pauses for Colton to identify the pet in the story.

"Alligator," says Colton.

"Sheesh. We're in the middle of Wisconsin and you pick alligator? Oh well. 'Old man, gold man' the children sang to him, and not nicely. They called him gold man because he had gold...,"

"Shoes," says Colton.

"Shoes? Okay. I was expecting teeth or hair or something. Shoes. His golden shoes gave him superpower privileges with his alligator. He could stand on the back of his alligator with those gold-enchanted shoes and fly up to the moonlight. He could go anywhere he wanted in a moment's notice. He boarded his old alligator buddy with his golden shoes and took off for..."

"Tahiti."

"And heads for Tahiti. When the alligator and old man gold man get to Tahiti, they look up someone that the old man gold man had known a really long time ago, but he hadn't seen in years. He visits..."

"His daughter."

"His daughter was being held captive in a castle chamber on the top floor. Only kind Tahitian servants looked upon her care, and brought her food and firewood for her cold, damp chamber. Thank goodness they took care of her. A Tahitian dwarf had joined the circus, and told old man gold man his daughter was in captivity. What could he do? How could he get her out? The Tahitian dwarf told him where the key was hidden. It was hidden..."

"In a jar of chili peppers."

Oh dear. Colton still has chili peppers on his mind as he's falling asleep. Poor guy. "The key was hidden inside a jar of chili peppers. So old man gold man flew to the kitchen cellar and found the jar of chili peppers and extracted the key. Then flew to the top of

46

the castle chamber and unlocked the door to free his beautiful daughter. She was so thankful she…"

"Kissed the alligator."

"She kissed the alligator and suddenly he transformed into a handsome young prince. He had been cast under a spell and wouldn't turn back to a handsome prince unless he had been kissed by a kind-hearted beautiful girl. But then he kissed her back in love and gratitude and she turned into an old hag with crooked yellow teeth and warts all over her face. 'Arrgh' cried the prince as he realized he hadn't been kissed by a real beautiful girl after all. He turned back into an alligator. 'Arrgh' cried the beautiful girl when she realized she had fallen for a spell and was punished by becoming an ugly hag. 'Arrgh' cried old man gold man when he realized that his daughter and his pet alligator were both bewitched. So he put his golden shoes on the back of the alligator and flew to…"

Nothing.

Nothing at all. Colton must have fallen asleep during the story. Oh well. Gus is tired too. He didn't realize how precious, or how little, sleep would be that night.

# Chapter 12

Bumbada...Bumbada...Bum!   Bum!   Bumbada....Bumbada...
Bum! Bum!

What is that? Drums? Drums in the middle of the night in the middle of the woods? Is this a dream or a nightmare?

Bumbada...Bumbada...Bum!   Bum!   Bumbada....Bumbada...
Bum! Bum!

Now awake, and realizing this is not a dream, Gus shakes Colton. "Colton! What is that?"

"I don't know," as he rubs his sleepy eyes. "Drums?"

"Yeah, I guess." They both jump up and unzip the door of the tent and peer out, just heads sticking out. Ten feet away are four men in dark clothing. The drum beat stops. All is quiet.

"Colton and Gus, you have been called forth by the King of the Studly Brotherhood to stand trial for crimes against not being studly enough. How do you plead?"

"Sheesh. It's Deuce, and that's Jake with the drum." The other two are cousins, the other Aunt Sis' boys. They walk out of the tent but grab the sleeping bags to wrap around like blankets, they're sleeping in their regular clothes.

"Knock it off Deuce," Colton says as he zips back up the tent flap.

"Keeping out a scourge of mosquitoes?" Gus makes a play on his new vocabulary word as he sees Colton zipping up the tent door. So far they think this is fun—or funny.

Colton nods at Gus, and turns his attention to his older brother and cousins.

"You're not the king of anything, Deuce. Zach is the head of the Studly Brotherhood anyways."

"Jake, I never knew you were so talented with a drum," Gus says with a smile.

Deuce looks a little crazed as he comes forward and grabs Colton and starts walking toward the creek, yanking on his ear to force him to follow. "Come on Jake, grab your dweeb of a brother."

"Ow!" cries Colton. "Knock it off, Deuce, that hurts!"

"Baby!" Deuce yells back at Colton. "You're such a baby."

"Hey, knock it off!" Gus yells, trying to protect Colton from Deuce.

"What's going on Deuce?" Jake asks, confused about the turn of events. "We've had our fun and woken up the boys. Let's go." But Deuce is still walking toward the creek—dragging Colton, and not listening to his cousins. They run along to catch up, not sure what Deuce is up to.

"For crimes of being total dweebs," carries on Deuce by the edge of the creek. "Pete and Repeat will undergo water torture." Deuce laughs an evil laugh.

Colton thrashes, trying to break free, and succeeds for a second. Deuce lunges after him and grabs him by the shirt. He's so much bigger he tosses him like a rag doll, and Colton falls on top of his fly rod that was leaning against the tree, snapping it in half. He doesn't have any time to lament its loss, as Deuce has both hands on him now. With a hard shove he propels his little brother, with sleeping bag tangled around his right foot, into the cold creek. Both boy and bag sink to the mucky bottom.

"Stop it!" Gus yells out, and reaches for Colton, but Deuce shoves him back.

Deuce steps forward and dunks Colton, holding him down until Deuce decides to let him up. Probably only a second, but a second that seems to last forever.

"Deuce—KNOCK IT OFF!" Jake comes over and shoves his older cousin. "Enough. That's not funny!"

The look on Colton's face as he breaks through, sputtering muddy water is fear, raw fear. He crawls through the mud to the safety of the grass bank, drenched and tangled in a wet sleeping bag, not sure if it's over or not.

"Your turn, Jake."

Jake turns to leave. "You gotta be kidding me. Forget it, Deuce," calls Jake over his shoulder, on his way out. "They're just kids. Leave 'em alone. I'm sorry, Colton. Come on, guys." Jake and the other two cousins leave. Deuce can't let it go.

"Dweebs!" he snarls at the boys, and shoves Gus into the water, too. He doesn't dunk Gus and hold him down like he did with Colton, but he walks away, calling them names under his breath.

# Chapter 13

"You okay?" Gus looks over at Colton. "Let's build a fire and dry off." Gus heads back to the fire pit and reloads it with kindling. He looks back and Colton hasn't moved. "Come on buddy, come over by the fire. I'll just get it going."

He spies the gas can about 30 feet away, and is tempted, but just for a moment. He's not that desperate, although he is sloshing around in wet blue jeans and soaking wet socks. He finds small, thin sticks and loads them in the bottom of the pit. He snaps off the dead pieces that cling to the bottom of pine trees, even picks up a few pine needles. Soon the fire is started and he walks back over by Colton. He's just sitting there: soaking wet, looking like an orphaned kitten, shivering, next to his broken fly rod.

"Come on, Colt. I've got a nice fire started. Let's dry off and warm up." Gus grabs at his arm and Colton jerks it back, startled out of his brief catatonic state.

"I hate him. I hate him! I HATE HIM!" Colton throws a fit, punching at the air, wildly; ending up a sobbing puddle. Gus gives him a minute to let it all out. Then he gently leads him, this time without protest, over to the fire. Colton sits on one of the bench logs. He's shivering cold and his lips are blue. "Take off your wet clothes." Gus walks back into the tent, slips out of his wet and dirty socks before stepping inside, and fishes out pajamas from both of their backpacks. They had them packed but never changed into them, having slept in their clothes.

"Put these dry pajamas on." Colton hasn't moved and is just sitting there, shivering. "I'm going to put mine on, see?" Gus throws off his wet stuff and it feels really good to put dry pajamas on. Colton's still sitting there, spent from both the fight with Deuce and his tirade.

"Come on," Gus keeps encouraging. "It feels so much better." Finally he snaps out of it and whips off his wet clothes with disgust, punishing the nearest tree trunk, and puts on the dry pajamas. Colton's sleeping bag is soaking wet, and Gus hangs it on a tree branch close to the fire to dry out.

Gus adds a lot of dry wood to get the fire burning hot and bright. It feels good and eventually the boys warm back up. Colton's no longer shivering with blue lips, but he's still steaming mad. Gus had no idea that Colton was tormented so much. What will they say tomorrow when the family's all together for Deuce's party?

Gus and Colton don't say anything about the Studly Brotherhood attack on the campground the next day. No apology from the older boys, either. Gus is sure that Zach would not approve—at all. He probably doesn't know. Zach created the Brotherhood to make the boys a close-knit family and have each other to turn to when they needed someone. Deuce has totally changed it. Who would have thought you need help from within your own family?

Colton shoots daggers of dirty looks at Deuce the entire day— all through church and during his party. His mom doesn't know what's going on, she just thinks Colton's got an attitude problem. Annie's not sure what's going on either, and Gus is not going to tell them—at least not yet.

On Monday morning they go their separate ways. Annie and Jake go back home and to work, leaving really early. Jim has a project in Wisconsin and Gus is invited along.

"Thanks, Rich. See you tomorrow. Thanks for being flexible." Jim hangs up his cell and turns to Gus, as the car kicks up dust on the gravel driveway heading to the main road. "Okay, I moved Monday's appointment to Tuesday. Something's come up in Fond du Lac. Ready to rock and roll?"

"Sure," Gus replies, excited for a trip with his dad. "What's the plan?"

"There's a photo op at Mercury Marine," says Dad. "I think you might have fun being along on this one. We'll do the thing for today, tomorrow instead."

"Photo op? What's the story?"

"A special visitor that they want me to capture with the camera. Let's go."

Little did Gus realize how special this special visitor would turn out to be.

# Chapter 14

Gus is a little worried about Colton and Deuce as they leave the farm. Jake told Gus that he talked to Zach about it. Hopefully things will be better once Zach weighs in, but it's hard to know. Gus saw a side of Deuce that he didn't like. Poor Colton has to live with it every day. At least Deuce is heading off to college in August. Maybe he'll grow up and appreciate his family when he's away at school.

Gus and his dad enjoy a little windshield time enroute to Fond du Lac. Windshield time is great because there isn't anything else going on to interrupt and there's plenty of time to talk. Sometimes about important things without anybody else listening or butting in with their two cents.

The two talk about trips coming up this summer and the baby coming in the fall. Dad's honest and tells Gus that he was surprised when he found out. They hadn't exactly planned it—whatever that means. So he understands that the idea can take a little getting used to. "This baby," Dad continues while driving, "is really a blessing for our family. It might not have been exactly what we were thinking of as perfect timing or perfect spacing for our kids, but sometimes, well…most of the time really, God knows better what we need than we do. I think we're lucky and blessed to have a baby coming our way."

"I'm getting used to the idea. I probably changed yours and Mom's world when I came along, didn't I?"

"You sure did, Gus," answers Dad. "Jake's too. Jake was already in Kindergarten when you came along so we started over again with the whole baby thing. And we'll do it again."

"Do you know what you'll name her?"

"No, not yet," answers Dad. "Do you have an idea?"

"I've been thinking about it. I'll let you know if I come up with a good one. Okay?"

"Okay," says Dad. "Deal." Gus tells him about what happened with Deuce and the boys in the middle of the night. Gus doesn't want to get Jake in trouble, but he also doesn't want to keep it a secret. Based on Jim's reaction, it sounds like Deuce crossed the line.

"Deuce needs a little more correction in his life," says Dad. Gus is certain his folks have figured out that part of parenting. They keep a close eye on both boys, and there will be consequences if they mess up along the way. But they're never mean and would never hurt either one of them. That doesn't mean they don't get their point across, though.

Conversation shifts to the newest batch of Studly root beer that Dad is planning. He plays around with brewing home-made root beer for the Fourth of July festivities, trying different recipes and taste testing to see which one everyone likes the best. There's always a crowd at the Roberts house for that holiday, and home-made root beer along with Grandpa Bud's home-made ice cream is a real treat, especially when you put them together for a root beer float.

Arriving in Fond du Lac at the security gate, Jim and Gus check in for a visit with Shelly Fishburn. She's Dad's contact for PR at the company—PR is public relations. It's the same kind of stuff that Annie does for the Minnesota Twins. Shelly hires Jim when she needs a good photographer.

They get badges to clip on their shirts, then park in visitor parking in front of the building. In the lobby they wait for Shelly, along with a couple of big motors on display.

"Are these doors locked?" Gus asks his dad, looking at several doors that lead from the lobby in different directions.

"Yes they are," he answers.

"Why do they have to lock their office?"

"I can think of a few reasons. One is that they don't want stuff to get stolen, so people can't just walk in or out without supervision."

"How can you steal an engine, Dad?"

"People steal all sorts of things, sad as that truth is," replies Dad. "Some people might steal parts and props. They could be small enough to walk out with. Besides, another thing people steal is information."

"Like cheating by reading an answer off someone else's test?"

"Yeah, like that," answers Dad. "They don't want another company to see any of the information they have about new products or new promotions or even pricing and cost of goods. All that information is top secret."

Shelly arrives. She's very tall and very pretty. "Hi Jim, and Gus, if I remember right," she says to them both. Dad probably told her he was along on the phone.

"Hi, Shelly," Jim answers, and shakes her hand, very professionally. Gus gives it a try, too, but it still feels a little awkward to shake hands like an adult. Gus wants to get to know Shelly Fishburn, though, and really well. She's in charge of who's on their pro-staff and one day he wants to be on Mercury's pro-staff.

"Come on back to the conference room," she says as she holds her security pass up to the pad next to the door. It beeps and the light turns green and all three walk through the open door. "Thank you for coming so quickly. We got word yesterday that Kevin was going to be here and we wanted to get it into our dealer and employee magazine. We have only a couple of days before it goes to press, so we can slip it in if we hurry."

"No problem, glad it worked out that I was nearby and available," answers Jim. Gus doesn't say anything. He knows that when parents are working and kids are along they just need to be quiet and polite. Answer questions that are asked, but otherwise, silence is golden. They walk into a conference room and Gus cannot believe his eyes.

# Chapter 15

"Jim, I think you've met Kevin VanDam before," says Shelly. "Kevin, this is Jim's son, Gus. You'll need to watch out for Gus, he's planning to take your spot as the world's best angler one day."

"All right, Gus," says Kevin. "Bring it on, dude." And they all laugh. Except Gus. He forgets to breathe and is down on the floor in a heap in 2.5 seconds. When he wakes up everyone is standing over him, asking if he's okay.

Gus sits up, and looks at Kevin VanDam standing next to him. He wasn't dreaming. "This is kind of embarrassing," Gus says softly. "I mean, I'm such a big fan of yours Mr. VanDam. You are the most amazing angler...ever!" Gus stands up, slowly.

"Call me Kevin, Gus, please." Gus looks a little woozie again.

"If Gus is okay let's get going on this photo shoot," as Shelly keeps moving things along. "Kevin only has about two hours before he has to leave for the airport."

The three adults talk while they walk back to another room. Gus follows behind and the workers in the office are waving and saying hello to Kevin as he walks by. He waves back and says "hi" most of the time. Some of them he knows by name and he makes sure to use it. He's a nice guy. That's a big part of Kevin VanDam's success story—good fisherman plus nice guy. If Matt Driver were a great fisherman, people would not want to follow him and watch him on TV, or even Gus' cousin Deuce. They'd just be jerks or bullies that are great fishermen. But a nice guy that's a good fisherman? That's the ticket.

Gus realizes that he wants to be like that—he can't help it. He's always wanted people to know him as an amazing fisherman. That's why they love Kevin VanDam. He's won so many tournaments—and big important championships, too. Five time Bassmaster Classic Champion. He's won more than four million dollars fishing tournaments and that doesn't count endorsements or anything else. He knows how to catch fish. No matter what the conditions, and no matter who he's fishing against, he knows how to put fish—usually the *right* fish—in the boat. He's a really nice person in addition to being a great fisherman.

Today Gus realizes that he can do it. Kevin did it, he can do it, too. It makes him even more excited about fishing in the professional team tournament in September with his dad. The next step in building his name and accomplishments.

Jim takes lots of pictures from a lot of different angles. They head out to the factory line where the motors are made and the guys and gals working on the motors stop to shake Kevin's hand when he walks by. It's like a party and Jim grabs pictures of Kevin VanDam with the Mercury employees. They're so happy to see him and meet him, and proud he's a Mercury guy. Soon, about 40 or so gather, and someone shuts off the overhead line that carries the motors from spot to spot. Then he addresses them as a group.

"You guys should be really proud of the work that you do here," Kevin says to the employees. "You make a great product and it's one that I depend on every day. And it isn't only for people like me that make their living fishing. It's also for folks like Gus over here, that enjoy fishing for the fun of it, too." Kevin motions for Gus to come on over, and he gets to stand right next to him. A lot of the people say "hi" to Gus and "welcome to Mercury" as he walks to the front by Kevin.

"A boat and motor are for fun, of course," Kevin continues talking to the employees. "Fishing is supposed to be fun. We all have to remember that. The day it stops being fun is the day I stop doing this. I love to fish." Sounds kind of familiar to Gus. He loves to fish, too!

"But a dependable motor is about safety, too," Kevin continues. "When your engineers design a great motor and you folks on the line build it with care and quality; that means I have a motor that won't leave me stranded on Lake Erie or Green Bay when a blow picks up and getting in becomes a matter of life or death. And if I want to take precious cargo, like my family on the water (like a lot of you do on weekends), we all want a motor that's going to get us back safely. Thank you for what you do. Seriously, thank you."

Jim snaps a lot of photos and they move along, eventually back to the conference room where everything started. Shelly needs to drive Kevin to the Milwaukee airport and Jim needs to download the photos to his laptop to review them and pick the best ones to look over with Shelly when she gets back.

"Dad, can I ride along to take KVD to the airport?" Gus says it in a whisper, so that if his dad doesn't like the idea, he won't be embarrassed about saying it out loud. "I promise I'll be good and quiet as a church mouse and will remember the golden rule: think first, talk second."

Dad laughs and nods. Gus loves it when his dad laughs. He walks over to Shelly and asks if it would be okay.

"Sure," she answers, looking at Kevin who nods in affirmation. "You can ride along and keep me company on the way back from Milwaukee. I'll be glad for someone to talk to."

"Do I have a second to get something from the truck?"

"Okay," says Shelly. "Let's grab it on the way out." Gus gets the keys from his dad and the trio walks out to her truck.

Gus unlocks Jim's vehicle and grabs his St. Croix rod from the back. He sits in the back seat and Shelly and Kevin talk all the way to the airport. When they stop at the curb, Gus gets out of the truck when Shelly and Kevin do.

"Mr. VanDam, I'd like to give this to you as a gift," Gus says as he presents his St. Croix rod.

"Gus, this is really nice of you, but I just can't," he says. Gus' heart sinks. He wants him to have this, even though he kind of wants to keep it for himself too. Dilemma.

"How about you keep it for a spare?"

"Listen," he says as he gets out a black marker from his briefcase. "I have an idea. Why don't you and your dad come visit me and my boys and we'll all go fishing together, the five of us. You guys can get over to Michigan sometime this year?" He says this while he signs the cork handle of Gus' rod.

"That would be so great!" Gus gets that woozie feeling again, but remembers to breathe this time and stays upright. Kevin hands Gus a business card and puts his cell phone number on it. "Give this to your dad," he continues. "But don't give that number out okay? Let's keep that just between us."

"Top secret, you got it. I'll look forward to that day like Christmas!"

Kevin laughs. "Sounds good. Shelly, good to see you as always. Take care of business." Then he leaves.

Gus moves up to the front seat of Shelly's truck and they pull away from the airport on the journey back to Fond du Lac. "You hungry?" she asks.

"Yes. I think I worked up an appetite meeting Kevin VanDam."

Shelly smiles. "Let's stop for a bite to eat." They pull into a Culver's and she orders a salad and Gus gets a butter burger with cheese basket and a root beer.

They talk about Shelly's two boys. They're very lucky and get to go to fun places sometimes—like big fishing tournaments and shows. They met Kevin VanDam before, but they didn't faint.

"Promise you won't tell anyone that I fainted when I met Kevin VanDam?"

Shelly gives him a look as her cell phone goes off. Gus pushes it a little harder. "Pinky promise?" She links her right-hand pinky to his, her smooth white skin with bright pink fingernails next to his darker skin, with fingernails that look like he was four-wheeling in the mud all weekend. She smiles as she answers her phone, letting go of Gus' pinky.

Her cell phone rings constantly on the drive back. She's done with one phone call and then another one comes. She didn't need Gus to keep her company on the drive, she has lots of people to talk to.

When they arrive at Mercury's offices, Jim has finished with his photos and he and Shelly look over his file of favorites. She's happy. There are several photos that she likes that will work for the article and he hands her a jump drive so she can copy the photos to her computer. She walks back to her office with the jump drive. Dad and Gus have a moment alone.

"I bet you're hungry," says Dad. "You probably need some lunch."

"We stopped at Culver's, so I'm okay. But I bet you're hungry."

"I'm starving. Let's grab something to eat."

"No problem for me. I'm a growing boy, I can eat two lunches in one day."

Shelly brings the jump drive back and gives it to Jim with her thanks. Now, on to the appointment that Jim moved from Monday to Tuesday to fit this trip to Mercury in. The two are back in his truck, heading north.

"You could have warned me, Dad." Gus is riding shotgun, Jim pulling onto route 41.

Jim laughs. "That was half the fun, Gus. You were totally caught off guard."

"No kidding. I loved meeting Kevin VanDam. He's so amazing. I don't think there's ever been a better fisherman—ever."

"I got some great photos of the two of you together."

"Cool."

"And you got his autograph?"

"Oh yeah, on my rod. And an invitation to go fishing with him and his boys in Michigan. Here's his card. He said to keep the cell phone number just between us." Gus hands Jim the card from his pocket.

"That would be really fun. Hopefully we can do it one day." Jim smiles as he puts the card in the cup holder of his truck.

"What a day. This was amazing." Gus breathes a big sigh, a sigh full of contentment and happiness. "Where are we going now?"

"Park Falls, Wisconsin. About a four hour drive from here."

"Okay," Gus answers, thinking Park Falls, Wisconsin sounds familiar. "Wait, isn't that where…"

"Bingo, you got it. It's the home of St. Croix rods!"

# Chapter 16

"Oh my gosh, Dad. I almost gave my St. Croix rod away a little while ago."

"What?"

Gus explains his offer of his favorite rod to Kevin VanDam. "But he wouldn't take it. Man, I would feel horrible if I gave my favorite rod away and then we go to the home of St. Croix rods and I don't have one anymore. At least now, when we get there, I can say that I have one."

"And are pretty proud of it."

"Oh yeah. That was the best Christmas present ever."

"I hear they have a bin in the corner of the store with really good deals. Stuff that they refurbish is marked way down."

"Cool. But I'm saving up money for our tournament in September. I don't have any extra money these days."

"Not even for a great deal?"

"Nope. Won't do me any good to have extra rods if I don't have a place to use them—like a tournament."

"You're taking this pretty seriously, Gus. You know—we might not cash a check at that tournament at all, let alone win it."

"I don't know, Dad. I think you need a little more confidence."

Jim laughs. "There's confidence…and then there's cocky. Big difference."

"What's the difference."

"Confidence comes from the hard work that you know what you're doing and have a good shot at putting a great plan together. Cockiness is…I don't know…it's hard to explain. A cocky guy thinks that because of who he is, he deserves to win."

"I'm working on a plan, Dad. I'm researching Waubay online already. Will we have time for a trip out there before the tournament? Get some pre-fish in?"

"Maybe we could go the weekend before and have a full week to prepare."

"That would be great. I'm so excited to go to the headquarters of where they make St. Croix rods, Dad. Cool!"

Jim and Gus stay in a motel about a half-hour from Park Falls. In the morning they arrive a few minutes early.

"Come on, let's check out the store for a little while," Jim suggests. They detour into the retail store to look around.

"Wow." Gus can't believe his eyes. Rows and rows of St. Croix rods, in different sizes and colors. Boxes of reels stacked up, some St. Croix and other brands, too. Hoodie sweatshirts, t-shirts, hats, and lots of lures and tackle, too. The 15 minutes they want to kill flies by too fast.

"Come on Gus, time for our meeting with Rich."

"Can we come back here afterwards? I'm not done looking yet."

"Sure, let's go." The two turn left outside the shop doors and proceed a few feet farther to the main office, down the sidewalk

"Good morning. I'm Jim Roberts and this is my son, Gus. We're here to see Rich Belanger."

"Please have a seat and I'll tell him you're here," she says. Gus can't sit down, he's too excited.

Rich walks out. "We're so glad you could both be here today. Come on back to the break room. We have everything ready." They walk past a few cubes and offices and head into a very busy lunch room. There are people packed in there, it looks like they're interrupting a big meeting.

"Let's hear it for Gus," someone shouts. "Hip, hip, hooray!"

"Hip, hip, hooray," the whole group echoes back. And again, "Hip, hip, hooray!"

Gus looks at his father with a look that says—What is this? He gives him a look back that says—I don't know, go with it.

A bit bewildered and awestruck, Gus walks numbly into the front of the room, with Rich leading the way. The people applaud and pat Gus on the back as he walks by, and some of the guys shake his hand. Older ladies pinch his cheek and tell him he's adorable. A couple of them even give a kiss and a hug.

Gus spies a big cake decorated with a fishing rod with a nice big fish on, and it says 'Welcome Gus Roberts' in script frosting. "Holy cow. What's going on here?"

"Gus, we invited you here today for this little celebration to say thanks," says Mr. Belanger. "We saw your photo on opening weekend in the Minneapolis Sunday paper and heard what you said on the TV interview for the news. And we couldn't be happier than to welcome you into the St. Croix rod family."

"Wow. This is for me?" Everybody claps their hands.

"So we tricked you into thinking you were coming up with your dad for a photo shoot, but really, we invited you up to say thank you, have some cake with all your new friends here, and see how St. Croix rods are made and what makes them so special. You already know they are great rods. Now you'll learn why."

Gus can't find his words. He's not usually shy or anything but this is a little over the top, even for Gus. He gives his dad a look that says—Help?! He gives him a look back that says—Manners!

"Thank you everyone," is all he can think of at first. "Thank you for this nice cake and for inviting me here today." Everyone is looking at him. He's a little nervous, but he keeps on going, prompted by Jim's smile. "It's no surprise to you guys here that I love my St. Croix rod, and that I love to fish." Everybody laughs. "I can't wait to see how you make these rods."

"That's what we'll do," Mr. Belanger continues. "Gus, on behalf of the entire St. Croix rod family, we hereby add you to the official pro-staff of St. Croix rods." They all clap. Mr. Belanger hands Gus a hoodie sweatshirt with the St. Croix logo and underneath it says— PRO-STAFF. It's official! Immediately and proudly, he puts it on. It's a little big, but he doesn't care—or notice.

Gus didn't know how cool today was going to be when he got up this morning.

# Chapter 17

Gus is so proud to wear his pro-staff hoodie, even though it's hot outside, he keeps it on. He feels ten feet tall. Can this really be true? One of his biggest dreams has just become reality. He's on the pro-staff of St. Croix rods!

"This is where we store the carbon fiber material," informs Mr. Belanger as he begins the tour in the back of the building, handing out safety glasses for everyone to wear. "Even though it looks like big black chunks of material, these piles are actually thin sheets on top of each other. Do you notice anything special about this room?"

"It's cold in here," Gus answers.

"Right. We keep it cool because the carbon fiber is impregnated with resin." They walk out of the cool storage room to a corner where a lot of long skinny metal sticks are stacked in groups. "These are the dies, or blanks, that are used to create a rod. The blanks are used over and over again, and you can see there are a lot of blanks of certain sizes." Some blanks are longer and thicker than others.

"These must be your best selling rods," Jim says, pointing where there are lots of the same size blanks.

"Right." They walk past a bunch of workers and go to another area in a different corner of the building. "Now in this area, George and Ron are cutting the carbon composite material to exactly fit the blank for the job," as Mr. Belanger points out that all visitors need to stand back from the yellow and black caution tape line that's drawn around the cutting table.

"Hi Gus, welcome aboard, buddy," says one of the guys working the cutting equipment.

"Thank you, sir." Wow. These guys all know Gus now.

"A computer is programmed to cut the material *exactly* to the specs for the rods. Years ago all the cutting was done by hand, but now it's all computerized." The material is laid out on the cutting table and air suction, kind of the opposite of an air hockey table, pulls the fabric tightly to the table. The guys smooth it out with their gloved hands. Then a big arm moves forward and back with a razor sharp cutter, slicing the carbon composite material into long triangles, resembling skinny tepees. The guys throw away the waste and then stack up the cut pieces.

"Now you know why you need to stand back from the yellow tape," adds Mr. Belanger. He's right because the cutting arm moves forward quickly and could whack a person standing too close.

They walk over to where some ladies are running an iron across the blanks and tacking the cut carbon fiber pieces to the heated rod die. They roll the cut composite material on the blanks, move it off to the side, then do it again, over and over. Then another guy takes the ones from their done pile and puts the blanks into a machine, it heats and rolls the blank so that the composite material is fused perfectly. There's baby powder everywhere. He works with gloves on and moves his finished blanks to a done pile, too.

Then another person takes them from there, and she wraps cellophane tape on them. A machine does it lickity-split. FFFFRRT! Wrapped. Just like that. But it takes a little while to get it lined up perfectly to get started.

The rods are placed in a tall oven and baked for two hours at 265 degrees. When the composite material is cool it's time to remove the blank so it can be used again. "Did you see Joe and the gals working with baby powder back there, Gus?" asks Mr. Belanger.

"Yes, sir. What is that for?"

"That's a tacking agent so that the carbon fiber doesn't stick to the rolling table. We also use a release agent to get the blank off the die, too. Pretty high tech, eh? Baby powder." Gus realizes that there's baby powder in his future. Kind of funny that it is used in making St. Croix rods. The blanks slip right out when they need them to. "After cooling the cellophane tape is removed."

"Wow, that's loud," Gus shouts over the noise of yanking off the tape.

"Yeah, that's the noisiest part of making a St. Croix rod," says Mr. Belanger. The workers wear hearing protection so it doesn't damage their hearing.

The rods are built a little bit longer than they need to be, so that they can be trimmed to the exact size. A computerized laser machine measures and cuts each one perfectly.

"Now each rod needs two more important checks before the next steps of finishing the rod. A sensitive machine checks the weight and diameter measurements before it goes to the rest of production, to make sure it is EXACTLY the right size. And a laser machine locates the straightest rotation of the rod and a person marks it for the guides that will be attached soon." Guides are the circle loops that the fishing line runs through. It takes lots of steps, and lots of people, to make these rods.

They walk to an area that looks like the art room at school. Paint splatters in dozens of colors are on every square inch of the floor, stairs and railings. The gals in this area wear paint splattered clothing to do their job, too. They dip the rods in paint and hang them up on a line. The rods travel through a dryer and come out the other side ready for the next phase. Some are blue, black, and red. They have lots of different colors, even pink and purple by the splatters on the floor.

"After the paint dries we move to where they attach the tips and guides. We put the rod in this machine to hold it and spin it, and using the marks from the laser earlier to attach the tip and guides so they all line up perfectly. Colored thread attaches each guide as it spins and then an epoxy is painted with a brush on the threads to hold them in place. But we can't let it sit there like that, or the glue drips. So we move the rod up to this drum that's rotating above." Mr. Belanger gives them a close-up look at all these steps, pointing at the machines and the drums that spin above their heads.

"Wow, there are a lot of rods on one of those drums," Gus notices.

"And a lot of drums," Jim adds.

"Yes, indeed. There are more than 30 rods around the outside of the drum, and they spin and spin until the epoxy is set. It can take a long time."

There are a lot of workers putting on guides and adding to their own drums above their heads. It looks interesting to stand back and see all the rods spinning high up in the air.

They move on to an area where guys work on attaching the shim for the reel seats. That makes a handle and a secure place to insert the reel. The shims are hollowed out to fit the exact rod dimensions so they slide in perfectly. Before the completed rods are packaged, a shiny coat of furniture polish is applied so they glimmer and sparkle. Now Gus knows a trick to keeping his St. Croix rod looking brand new—a little furniture polish.

"What do you think, Gus?" asks Mr. Belanger at the end of the tour. There are people giving one last look at the rods to make sure the guides and tips line up straight, the St. Croix logo decal is on correctly, and everything looks perfect before it leaves.

"I think it's amazing to see something like this." Jim gives Gus that look again. "Thank you very much for the tour today and learning all about how St. Croix rods are made. I enjoyed it very much, didn't you, Dad?"

"Yes, I did," answers Dad. "Thank you, Rich."

"And thank you for adding me to your pro-staff," Gus continues. "I always hoped you would one day, I didn't know it would be as a sixth grader!"

Mr. Belanger laughs. "Gus, you got us some great publicity and really showed what it's like to embrace our brand. That's all we ask from our pro-staff, to be ambassadors for the St. Croix brand. That means enjoying fishing yourself, teaching it to others and using quality products that work hard for your success in fishing. That's what we're all about here." Mr. Belanger is a great guy. "And next year when you and your dad start fishing some team tournaments together, we'll be proud to have you as a St. Croix pro-staffer on the tournament circuit."

"Actually, that reminds me of something."

# Chapter 18

The three walk through the 'employees only' door, into the store that Jim and Gus were in when they first arrived.

"Gus, just one more thing before you go," adds Mr. Belanger. "As a member of our pro-staff you get free equipment from time to time. And clothing," as he hands Gus a dark blue cap with St. Croix across the front. Gus puts it on immediately. With his sweatshirt and hat, he's flying the St. Croix colors for sure! "Today I'd like to invite you to pick out anything in the store that you want. Rod and reel combo of any preference. You pick."

"Holy cow!" Gus is like a kid in a candy store, except that he's a kid that loves fishing in a fishing rod store and gets to pick anything he wants. He can't believe it. "I don't know what to pick," he exclaims, looking at all the choices in the store. There really are hundreds and hundreds, where does he start?

"Look around a little bit and see what pops out at you," Dad says.

"Okay, let's see what jumps."

As he walks through the store Gus says a little prayer. His hands aren't folded and his eyes aren't closed, so it won't look to anyone else like he's praying, but he is.

*God, thank you for this amazing day. I didn't know all this was going to happen today and it has been a wonderful surprise. Thank you so much for all these really nice people here and for their hard work in the factory and putting me on the pro-staff. Help me to be a really good fisherman to show them that they made a good decision in me. I don't know what to pick here, so maybe you could help me a little bit. There are too many choices.*

*Mom says when I have tough decisions to make I should always ask for your help, so here goes. Help me with this one. Amen.*

"Tell me more about these rods, Mr. Belanger," Gus asks, looking at a particular display rack.

"Those are our fly rods and reels, for fly fishing. Ever done any fly fishing, Gus?"

"Yup, I was on Saturday at my cousin's place." Gus thinks for a moment about how much Colton likes to fly fish, and how Deuce caused all the trouble on Saturday night and Colton's rod got broken. It wasn't a fancy nice fly rod like a St. Croix, but still, his rod and reel got broken with the mean antics from his bully brother.

"I'll take this one." Dad and Mr. Belanger look a little surprised.

"Why that one, Gus?" asks Jim.

"Seems like a perfect rod." Colton will be really excited when Gus presents him with this new fly rod, a gift from a cousin that knows a little better about the trouble at home after this weekend. "Thank you so much, Mr. Belanger," Gus says while they are checking out at the cash register. Jim is buying a couple of rods from the bargain bin. "I can't wait for our first tournament this fall."

"This fall? You fishing something this year?"

"Yeah," Jim adds. "Gus talked me into the Masters on Waubay Lake in September. He'll just have turned 12 a week before the tournament, so he's eligible.

"Cool." Rich looks at Gus with a smile.

"I have to raise my half of the expenses for our team," Gus adds.

"You do?" Rich looks over at Jim, who shrugs his shoulders.

"Might as well teach him right away about risk and reward."

"How's it going so far?"

"I've got a job working for my neighbor doing yard work. She's just not giving me the hours I wanted, it's just every other week 9:30 to noon. I'll be more than half-way there by September."

"You know, as part of our pro-staff, we sometimes will help with portions of your entry fee," continues Mr. Belanger. "If you agree to fly the St. Croix colors on stage and in any photos."

"Could you really help, Mr. Belanger?"

Rich reaches over the counter for a yellow post-it note, and writes down a number. He folds the paper and passes it over to Gus. "We could contribute that amount."

Happiness washes over Gus. "That's perfect, Mr. Belanger. With my summer job and your help, I'll have my half for sure. THANK YOU." Gus wants to hug the man, not sure if that's okay. So he tries the more grown-up version of shaking hands. It feels a little awkward, but he'll have to get used to it.

Rich is glad that he can help. "You're welcome, Gus. I hope you do well and finish high."

"So do I, sir. So do I."

# Chapter 19

As Jim drives around Lake Minnetonka the sun is beginning to set and glistens off the lake. It's a beautiful evening and the weather is nice. There are a lot of boats on the water for a week night. Then again, it is the beginning of summer in Minnesota and everybody gets happy about beautiful days they can spend at the lake.

There's a thin layer of sand all across the driveway as they pull in, but the big pile is gone. Jake's been busy and his project looks complete from this side of the house.

Jake and Pops sit by a campfire on the beach. Annie's not home from a baseball game yet.

"Jakey and I decided we'd enjoy the sunset for a piece," exclaims Pops. Gus and Jim find them with a lemonade poured, listening to the game, now in extra innings on the radio.

The Roberts' home faces west and so watching the sunset is a part of their regular routine. In the winter the sun sets the farthest to the southwest, when the sun is at its lowest angle. As the days get longer the angle of the sun changes to due west—at both the spring and fall equinox. It moves the farthest northwest, the highest angle, by summer solstice, which is the longest day of the year and now only two weeks away. That means the sun is w-a-y to the northwest as they watch it set. The colors are red and almost pinkish-purple.

"The beach looks great," Dad offers to Jake. "Thanks for finishing."

"Sure," says Jake. He doesn't sound too happy to talk about it.

Gus grabs his St. Croix rod and show Pops and Jake where Kevin

VanDam signed it. They aren't nearly as excited as Gus wants them to be. And they didn't even notice his hat and sweatshirt. They probably think he bought it. They don't know.

Gus heads out to the end of the dock. A few casts are in order—to stay in practice and give himself a little space. He puts on a Dardevle spoon that'll cast as far as he possibly can, and reels in hoping for a nice big northern pike.

The deep dark green reflection of the trees on the water looks almost black as the sunset is nearly complete. With twinkling stars beginning to illuminate the night sky, Dad says, "Gus, time to call it a night."

"Okay, Dad," Gus answers. "One last cast." *Plunk* the sound of the Dardevle hits the water. The company that makes the red-and-white-striped spoon with the little devil imprint on it, Eppinger, spells it D-a-r-d-e-v-l-e. It's kind of an old-fashioned lure, but one that really catches nice fish, especially pike or musky. Pops was catching fish on Dardevle lures when he was a kid, so that tells you how long this lure's been around.

Thump. "Fish on," he says at first, just to himself. Then, louder, he calls to the guys at the campfire after he's given a good tug to set his hook. "Got a good one on the last cast of the night." A good hook set's needed to bring in another nice northern like last year. Whoa. It's a fighter as the scream of his drag fills the quiet night air. "What have you got?" Dad asks, as he brings the net, watching Gus work the fish.

"A northern pike or a musky, I think," Gus answers, already breathing hard. "A nice one."

"Better than the northern you got last year at this spot?"

"I think so," Gus replies, struggling to talk and work the fish at the same time.

If he pulls too hard he might break his line or his knot might come undone or the hook might snap. There's an important balance on bringing the fish in where you want it, but letting it have some line to relax and not fight quite so hard. Gus gives him a little, but then when he can, he reels in the line. S-t-e-a-d-y. Rod tip up. Whew, this is a good one.

"What line are you using?" Jim asks.

"Six pound mono. Wish I had braided on, but it's not."

Pops, Jake and Dad are all on the dock, watching Gus work this fish. This is so much work and fun mixed together. He's concentrating big time. "Which do you think, northern or musky?" Dad asks—AGAIN.

"I don't know." Gus hasn't caught a musky off the dock before—they're much harder to catch, of course. They call the musky the fish of 10,000 casts. "I don't think I'd be so lucky to have a musky while I was dinking around."

"Never know."

Northern pike and the musky are fairly close in the fish family. They both are big, mean competitors in the water. Both eat a lot of the smaller fish, and both have razor-sharp teeth. That's part of why they're hard to catch, they often cut the line with their teeth.

"Do you know how to tell the difference between a northern and a musky?"

"Well, yeah, they have a different body coloring."

"Yeah, but it can be tricky. Especially because they can crossbreed and that makes a hybrid. There's a sure way to know."

"Yeah?" Gus is listening, sort of. Mostly, he's focusing on bringing this big fish in.

"Turn the fish upside down and look at the underside of the jaw," Jim offers. "There are pores, small holes, on each side of the jaw. If there are five or fewer pores on each side, it's a northern pike. If there are six or more pores on each side, it is a musky."

Gus is in the kind of fight that he likes to be in, the kind he won't get grounded for. "You doing okay?" Dad, seriously now.

"Yeah, I'm okay. I'll be a lot better when I get this fish landed."

"You want me to help?" Jim asks.

"No way!" Yikes, he said that with a little edge. He'd better be careful or he'll be moving wheelbarrows of something, somewhere. He tries again. "No thanks, I got it." He finds a way to be polite.

And in a heartbeat it's gone. Gus knows before anyone else. Alone in the defeat for a moment.

"Aw...," he tells them as his line goes limp and all the fight is

74

gone. "I lost it."

There are 'aws' from everyone on the dock, even Jake. Darn. They didn't even get a look at it. Gus doesn't know if his trophy was a northern pike or a musky or a hybrid tiger musky.

"Next time," Jake says, as he pats his little brother on the shoulder and walks away. It's good that he doesn't tease Gus, or give him a hard time for losing the fish. Gus reels in his line and everything is gone—hook, line and sinker.

"Guess we'll have to stock up on some more Eppinger Dardevles, buddy-roo." Pops tries to lighten the moment. Pops and Jim head off the dock and sit back down by the fire, hearing the announcer wrap up the game.

"Aw, Twinkies lost. Darn." Pops groans.

They give Gus a minute to himself as he puts his rod away and joins them at the fire. It's dark now and the mosquitoes are out.

"I'm going to bed now," Gus' voice betrays the defeat he's feeling. He can't help it, frustrated that he lost that fish.

"Don't let it get your dauber down," says Pops, whatever that means.

"You'll get it next time," says Dad. "Do you think Kevin VanDam would get all down-in-the-dumps about letting a fish get away?"

*I do think Kevin VanDam would understand.* "Goodnight," he manages politely, although a part of him wants to throw a little tantrum. Sometimes, alone is better when you feel like this.

Gus brushes his teeth and puts on his Twins shorts and climbs into bed. The curtains flutter from the open window with a cool, night breeze. It feels good inside; comfy—with crisp sheets that smell like familiar laundry detergent. He looks over at the hoodie and cap on the hook and smiles, counting his blessings. *Wow. Am I really on the pro-staff of St. Croix rods?* Gus knows it won't take but a moment to fall asleep, so he hopes God will understand if his prayers are short tonight. So tired.

*Dear God: Thank you for everything…*

# Fishing Journal

## Learning About Rods and Reels

There are a lot of fishing rods and reels out there. How do you pick the right one? If you ever go into a tackle shop and walk around just looking at all the rods and reels, it would be easy to be totally confused.

Here are some rods and reels that you might like. They are the basics and give a great start. Put one on your birthday wish list or your Christmas list.

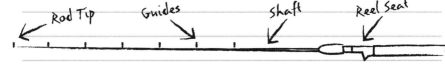

Guides are the circles that you put your line through. The rod tip is the guide at the top of your rod, the last one your line goes through. The main rod part that gives it length is the shaft. The part that you put your reel into, and usually connects to the handle, is called a reel seat.

Closed face spincast reels are THE BEST for beginners. The line spools behind a cover and you don't have a bail. Instead you have a rotor with one or two pins to catch your line and wind it on your spool. A push-button opens the pins on the rotor. There's usually a knob or screw that you can change the tension on the line. That's called drag. If your drag is loose a fish that takes the hook can easily pull line against you, if your drag is tight the fish can't pull the line against you very easily. If you set your drag too tight a fish can break your line more easily. If you set it too loose, it can be hard to get a fish reeled in. Dilemma. Set it in the middle at first and adjust as you go.

Drag

A spinning reel spools line in an open area with a bail. The bail is the part that you open or close to either let line out (open) or lock it (closed).

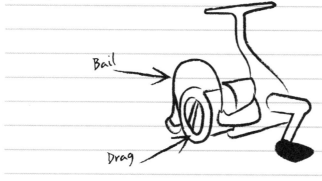

Bail

Drag

Baitcasting reels spool line behind a partial covering but you can still see most of the spool, and it has a release a little different than the spincast button. It still functions kind of like a button, though. Sometimes baitcasting reels have a line counter. That measures the feet of line that you let out, which helps to see how deep you're placing your baits. That is really helpful when trolling.

Line Counter

Yikes. Sometimes you can foul up the line in your reel. It's especially easy to do on a baitcasting reel and it turns into a birds nest. What a mess. Hey it happens. But it will happen less the more you practice and learn to control the line and your reel. Learn to adjust the spool tension so that when holding the rod straight out, the weight of the lure s-l-o-w-l-y lowers the lure to the water when you push the button. Then you're ready to cast. Use a light touch with your thumb to feather the release, so that as the lure is slowing toward the end of your cast, you are slowing the speed the line is coming off the spool. It's just a delayed reaction (another Newton's Law regarding inertia). My dad says adding warm water to the line after you spool it will allow the line to set to the size of your spool and not "remember" the bigger spool that it came from when you bought it. I haven't tried that, but my dad knows a lot of stuff about fishing, so I bet it helps.

Fly rods and reels are a little different. When you cast a fly rod you allow gravity and more laws of physics to pull your line away from the reel. It takes several sweeping motions to let enough line out to get to where you want to release it onto the water's surface. The fly reel doesn't have any kind of bail or button for closing or opening your line. It is always open but it does have drag settings.

When you fly fish, release line away from where you want to end up until you have enough line spooled out, then on your last cast, put it where you think the fish are. That way you won't scare the fish away before you are ready.

Ice fishing rods are much shorter. Usually 30 inches or less. They look like mini-spinning rods and usually use open face spinning reels.

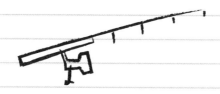

# Fish On Kids Books™

Gus' adventures continue throughout the
Fish On Kids Books Series. Buy them all!

If your club, team, troop or group is non-profit,
sign up to sell Fish On Kids Books to raise
needed cash for your program.

Fish On Kids Books
P.O. Box 3
Crystal Bay MN 55323-0003

Email: info@fishonkidsbooks.com
Web: www.fishonkidsbooks.com
Phone/Fax: (952) 472-1775